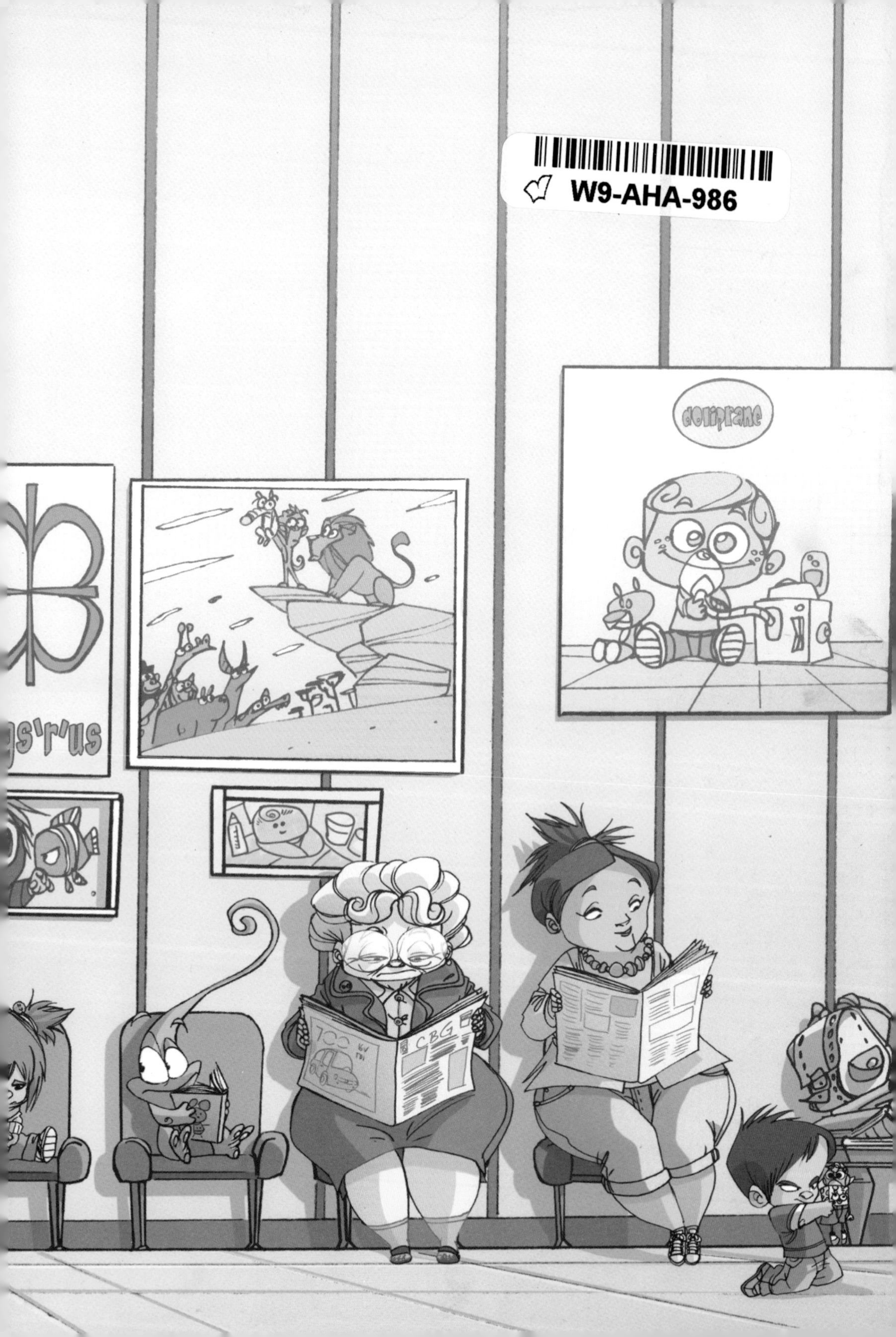
gs'r'us
CBG

Ernest & Rebecca

3

"Grandpa Bug"

Guillaume Bianco — Writer
Antonello Dalena — Artist
Cecilia Giumento — Colorist

PAPERCUTZ
New York

Mommy

She's the most beautiful mommy of all! She's not at home a lot because of her job, but she always finds time to cook my favorite food for me: "steak and fries with ketchup and mayonnaise!"

Daddy

He's an artist. A painter... like Picasso, but better! We have lots of fun together when mommy's at work... He's the funniest daddy of all!

Coralie

She's my big sister. I adore her, even if, ever since she's been in her rebellious stage, she stays in her room all the time.

Sam

He's my mom's fiancé. He's nice, but I'm suspicious he's really some kind of evil germ trying to contaminate our family unit.

Ernest

He's a microbe... and he's my best friend! I caught him one day while on a frog hunt. Since then, we're always together... He's super smart and really strong: he can change into anything!

And me: Rebecca!

I'm not very big... It's 'cause I hate soup! I'd rather eat ketchup and chase frogs with Ernest in the rain!

Ernest & Rebecca
#3 "Grandpa Bug"

Guillaume Bianco – Writer
Antonello Dalena – Artist
Cecilia Giumento – Colorist
Jean-Luc Deglin – Original Design
Joe Johnson – Translation
Janice Chiang – Lettering
Production – Nelson Design Group, LLC
Associate Editor – Michael Petranek
Jim Salicrup
Editor-in-Chief

© DALENA – BIANCO – ÉDITIONS DU LOMBARD
(DARGAUD-LOMBARD S.A.) 2011
www.lombard.com
All rights reserved.
English Translation and other editorial matter
Copyright © 2012 by Papercutz
ISBN: 978-1-59707-353-0

Printed in China
November 2012 by New Era Printing LTD.
Unit C, 8/F Worldwide Centre
123 Chung Tau St, Kowloon, Hong Kong

Distributed by Macmillan
First Papercutz Printing

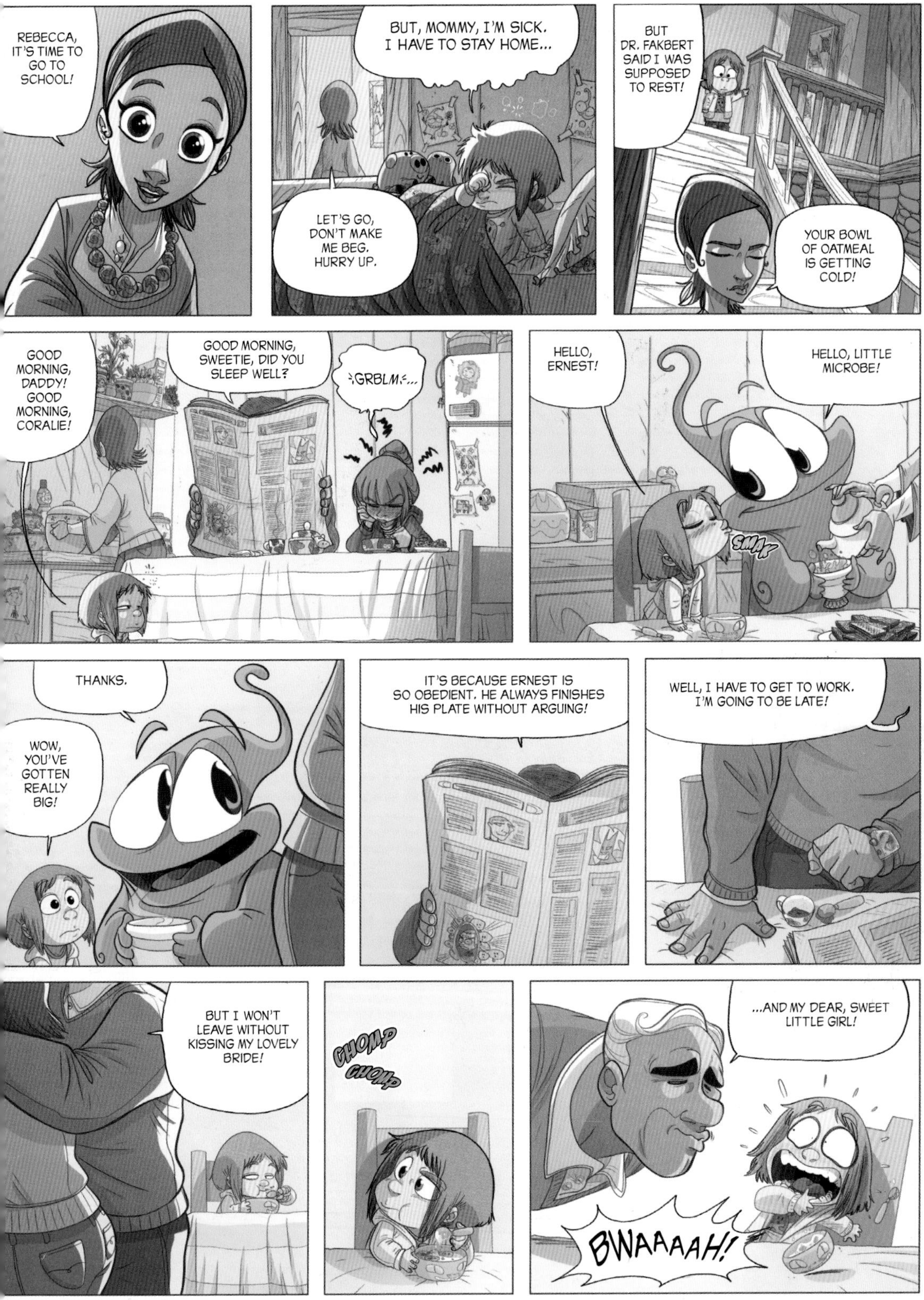
REBECCA, IT'S TIME TO GO TO SCHOOL!
BUT, MOMMY, I'M SICK. I HAVE TO STAY HOME...
LET'S GO, DON'T MAKE ME BEG. HURRY UP.
BUT DR. FAKBERT SAID I WAS SUPPOSED TO REST!
YOUR BOWL OF OATMEAL IS GETTING COLD!
GOOD MORNING, DADDY! GOOD MORNING, CORALIE!
GOOD MORNING, SWEETIE, DID YOU SLEEP WELL?
GRBLM...
HELLO, ERNEST!
HELLO, LITTLE MICROBE!
SMAK
THANKS.
WOW, YOU'VE GOTTEN REALLY BIG!
IT'S BECAUSE ERNEST IS SO OBEDIENT. HE ALWAYS FINISHES HIS PLATE WITHOUT ARGUING!
WELL, I HAVE TO GET TO WORK. I'M GOING TO BE LATE!
BUT I WON'T LEAVE WITHOUT KISSING MY LOVELY BRIDE!
CHOMP
CHOMP
...AND MY DEAR, SWEET LITTLE GIRL!
BWAAAAAH!

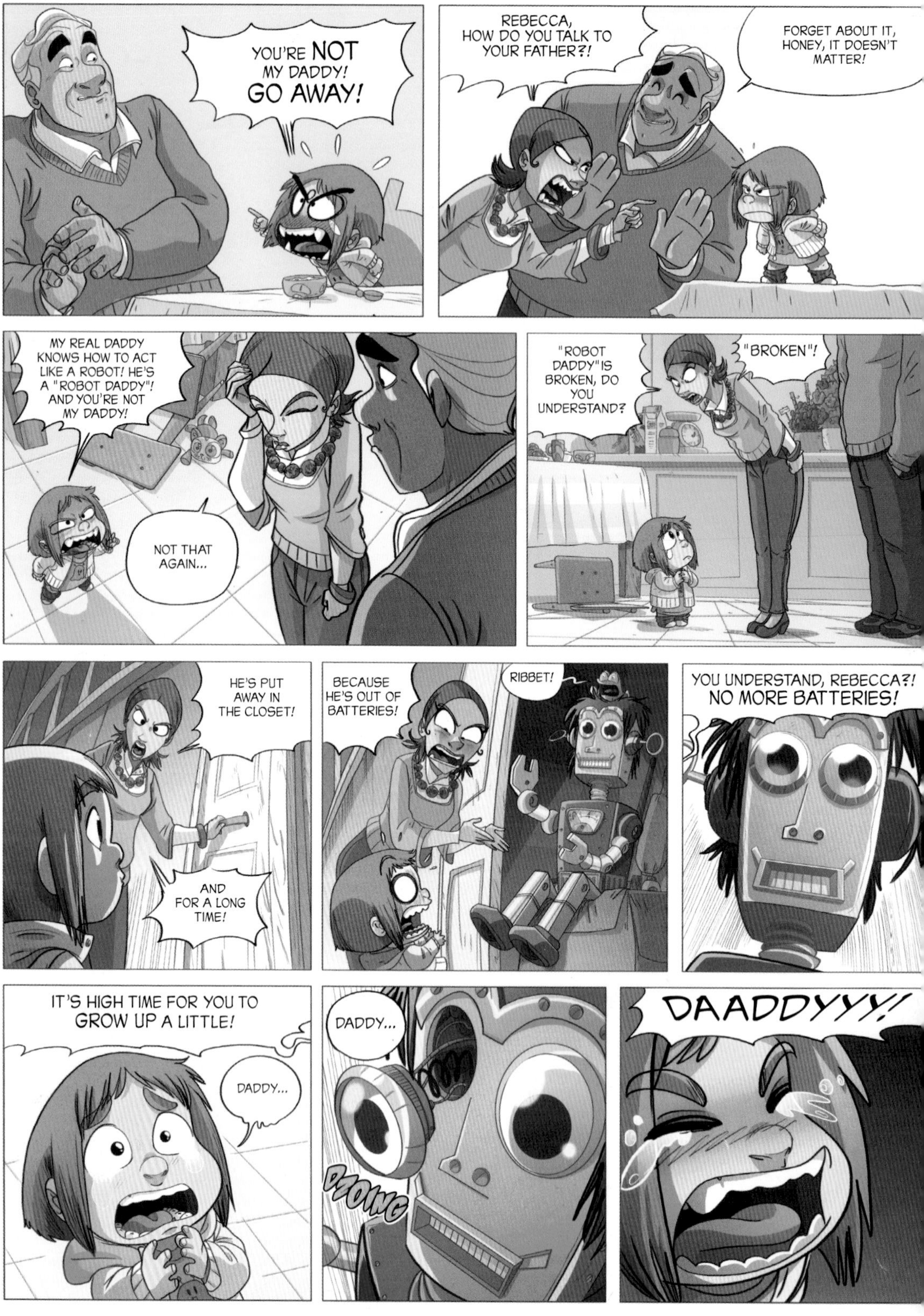
YOU'RE NOT MY DADDY! GO AWAY!
REBECCA, HOW DO YOU TALK TO YOUR FATHER?!
FORGET ABOUT IT, HONEY, IT DOESN'T MATTER!
MY REAL DADDY KNOWS HOW TO ACT LIKE A ROBOT! HE'S A "ROBOT DADDY"! AND YOU'RE NOT MY DADDY!
NOT THAT AGAIN...
"ROBOT DADDY" IS BROKEN, DO YOU UNDERSTAND?
"BROKEN"!
HE'S PUT AWAY IN THE CLOSET!
AND FOR A LONG TIME!
BECAUSE HE'S OUT OF BATTERIES!
RIBBET!
YOU UNDERSTAND, REBECCA?! NO MORE BATTERIES!
IT'S HIGH TIME FOR YOU TO GROW UP A LITTLE!
DADDY...
DADDY...
DZOING
DAADDYYY!

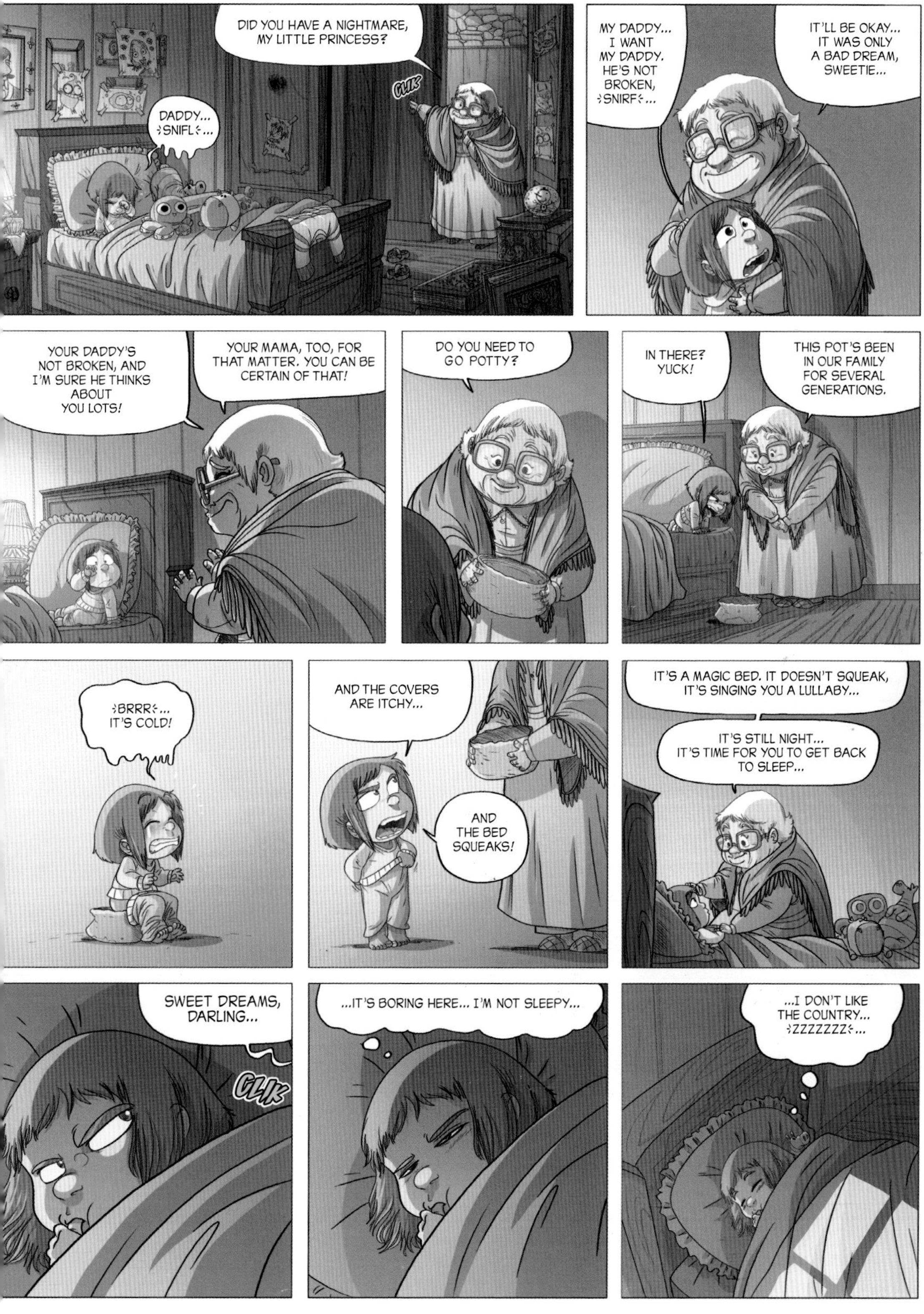
DID YOU HAVE A NIGHTMARE, MY LITTLE PRINCESS?
CLIK
DADDY... ⁝SNIFL⁝...
MY DADDY... I WANT MY DADDY. HE'S NOT BROKEN, ⁝SNIRF⁝...
IT'LL BE OKAY... IT WAS ONLY A BAD DREAM, SWEETIE...
YOUR DADDY'S NOT BROKEN, AND I'M SURE HE THINKS ABOUT YOU LOTS!
YOUR MAMA, TOO, FOR THAT MATTER. YOU CAN BE CERTAIN OF THAT!
DO YOU NEED TO GO POTTY?
IN THERE? YUCK!
THIS POT'S BEEN IN OUR FAMILY FOR SEVERAL GENERATIONS.
⁝BRRR⁝... IT'S COLD!
AND THE COVERS ARE ITCHY...
AND THE BED SQUEAKS!
IT'S A MAGIC BED. IT DOESN'T SQUEAK, IT'S SINGING YOU A LULLABY...
IT'S STILL NIGHT... IT'S TIME FOR YOU TO GET BACK TO SLEEP...
SWEET DREAMS, DARLING...
CLIK
...IT'S BORING HERE... I'M NOT SLEEPY...
...I DON'T LIKE THE COUNTRY... ⁝ZZZZZZZ⁝...

THE HOUSE MAKES NOISES...
THE WARDROBES CREAK... AND
THE SHUTTERS CLACK WITH
THE SLIGHTEST DRAFT...

OUTSIDE, NO NOISE, NO
CARS, NOTHING...

...JUST A STUPID, OLD ROOSTER
THAT CROWS THREE TIMES
AN HOUR...

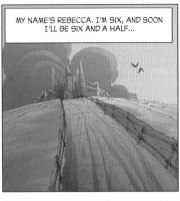

MY NAME'S REBECCA. I'M SIX, AND SOON
I'LL BE SIX AND A HALF...

BUT THERE'S NO USE REPEATING
THAT TO YOU. YOU ALREADY KNOW...

I'M ON VACATION AT GRANDPA BUG'S
AND GRANNY DOODLE'S...

IT'S ALREADY BEEN A WEEK,
AND I'M BORED TO DEATH HERE...
THERE'S NOTHING HERE...

MY DADDY AND MOMMY HAVE
SEPARATED... I MISS THEM. I'M DYING TO SEE
THEM AGAIN...

MY MOM HAS A NEW
FIANCÉ...

I'M SAD ABOUT
MY DADDY. HE'S
ALL ALONE...

...LIKE ME...

LUCKILY, TO KEEP ME COMPANY,
I HAVE A WONDERFUL FRIEND...
HIS NAME IS...

ERNESSsST!

WHERE
ARE
YOU?!

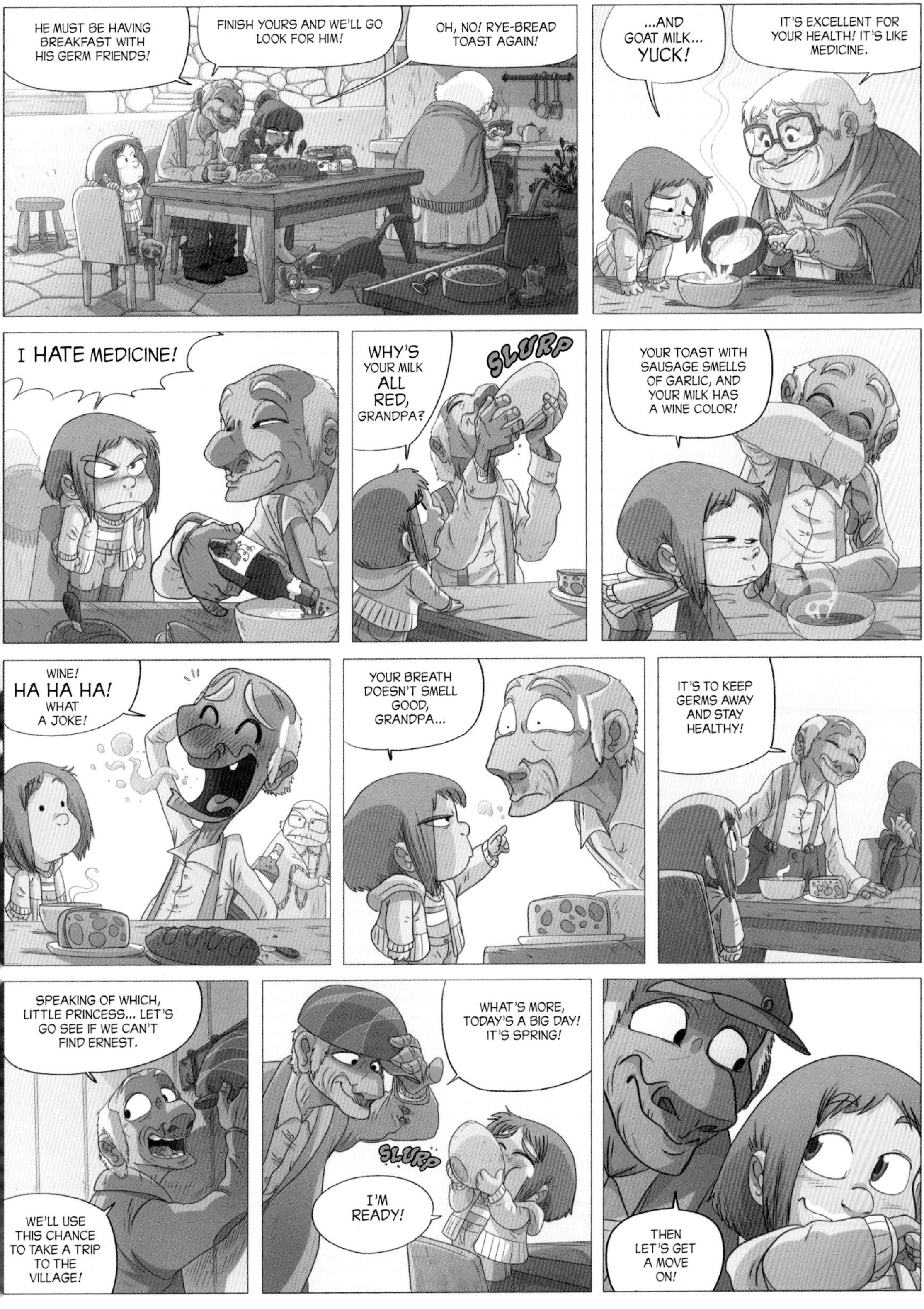
HE MUST BE HAVING BREAKFAST WITH HIS GERM FRIENDS!
FINISH YOURS AND WE'LL GO LOOK FOR HIM!
OH, NO! RYE-BREAD TOAST AGAIN!
...AND GOAT MILK... YUCK!
IT'S EXCELLENT FOR YOUR HEALTH! IT'S LIKE MEDICINE.
I HATE MEDICINE!
WHY'S YOUR MILK ALL RED, GRANDPA?
SLURP
YOUR TOAST WITH SAUSAGE SMELLS OF GARLIC, AND YOUR MILK HAS A WINE COLOR!
WINE! HA HA HA! WHAT A JOKE!
YOUR BREATH DOESN'T SMELL GOOD, GRANDPA...
IT'S TO KEEP GERMS AWAY AND STAY HEALTHY!
SPEAKING OF WHICH, LITTLE PRINCESS... LET'S GO SEE IF WE CAN'T FIND ERNEST.
WE'LL USE THIS CHANCE TO TAKE A TRIP TO THE VILLAGE!
WHAT'S MORE, TODAY'S A BIG DAY! IT'S SPRING!
SLURP
I'M READY!
THEN LET'S GET A MOVE ON!

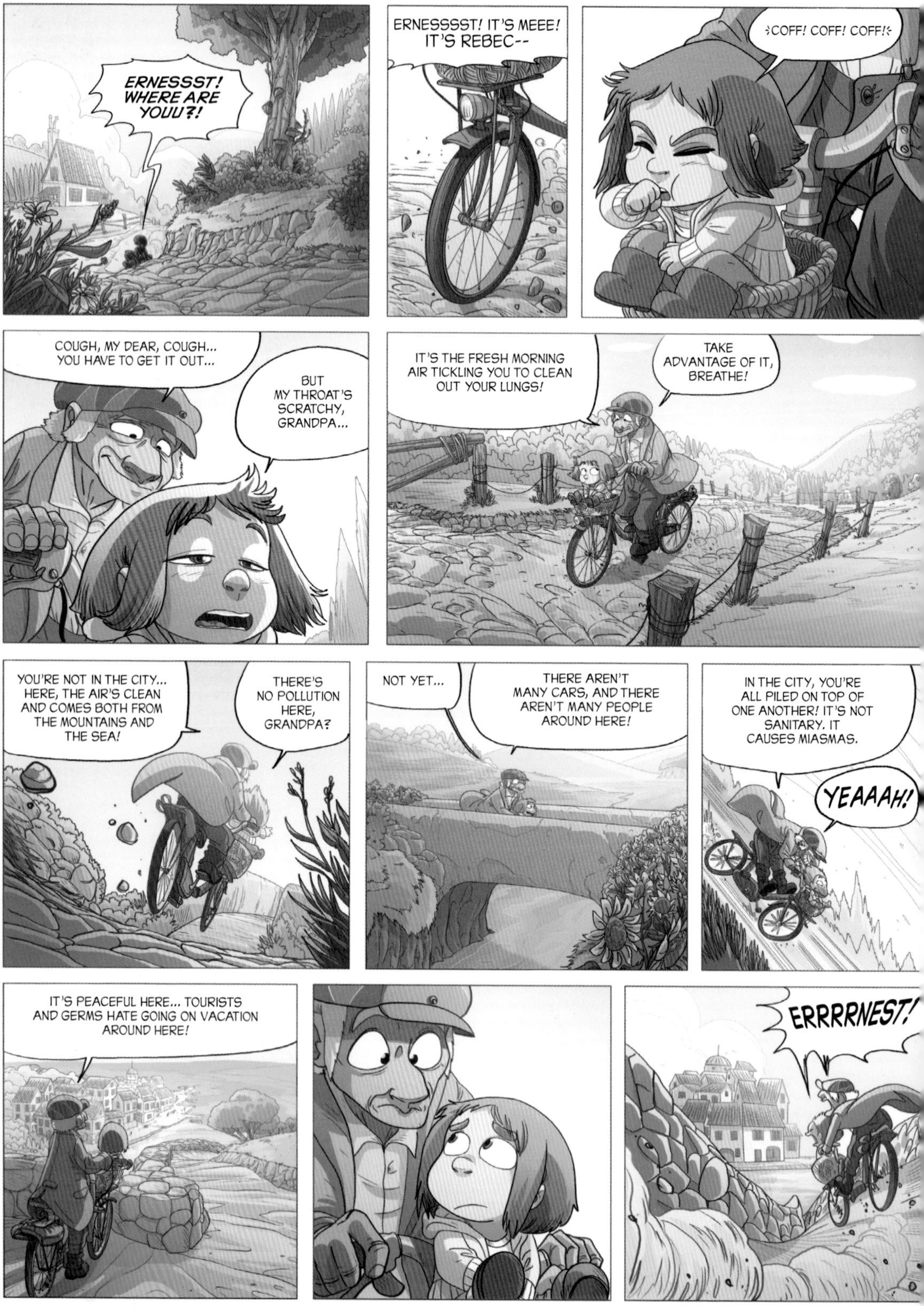

ERNESSST! WHERE ARE YOUU?!
ERNESSSST! IT'S MEEE! IT'S REBEC--
COFF! COFF! COFF!
COUGH, MY DEAR, COUGH... YOU HAVE TO GET IT OUT...
BUT MY THROAT'S SCRATCHY, GRANDPA...
IT'S THE FRESH MORNING AIR TICKLING YOU TO CLEAN OUT YOUR LUNGS!
TAKE ADVANTAGE OF IT, BREATHE!
YOU'RE NOT IN THE CITY... HERE, THE AIR'S CLEAN AND COMES BOTH FROM THE MOUNTAINS AND THE SEA!
THERE'S NO POLLUTION HERE, GRANDPA?
NOT YET...
THERE AREN'T MANY CARS, AND THERE AREN'T MANY PEOPLE AROUND HERE!
IN THE CITY, YOU'RE ALL PILED ON TOP OF ONE ANOTHER! IT'S NOT SANITARY. IT CAUSES MIASMAS.
YEAAAH!
IT'S PEACEFUL HERE... TOURISTS AND GERMS HATE GOING ON VACATION AROUND HERE!
ERRRRNEST!

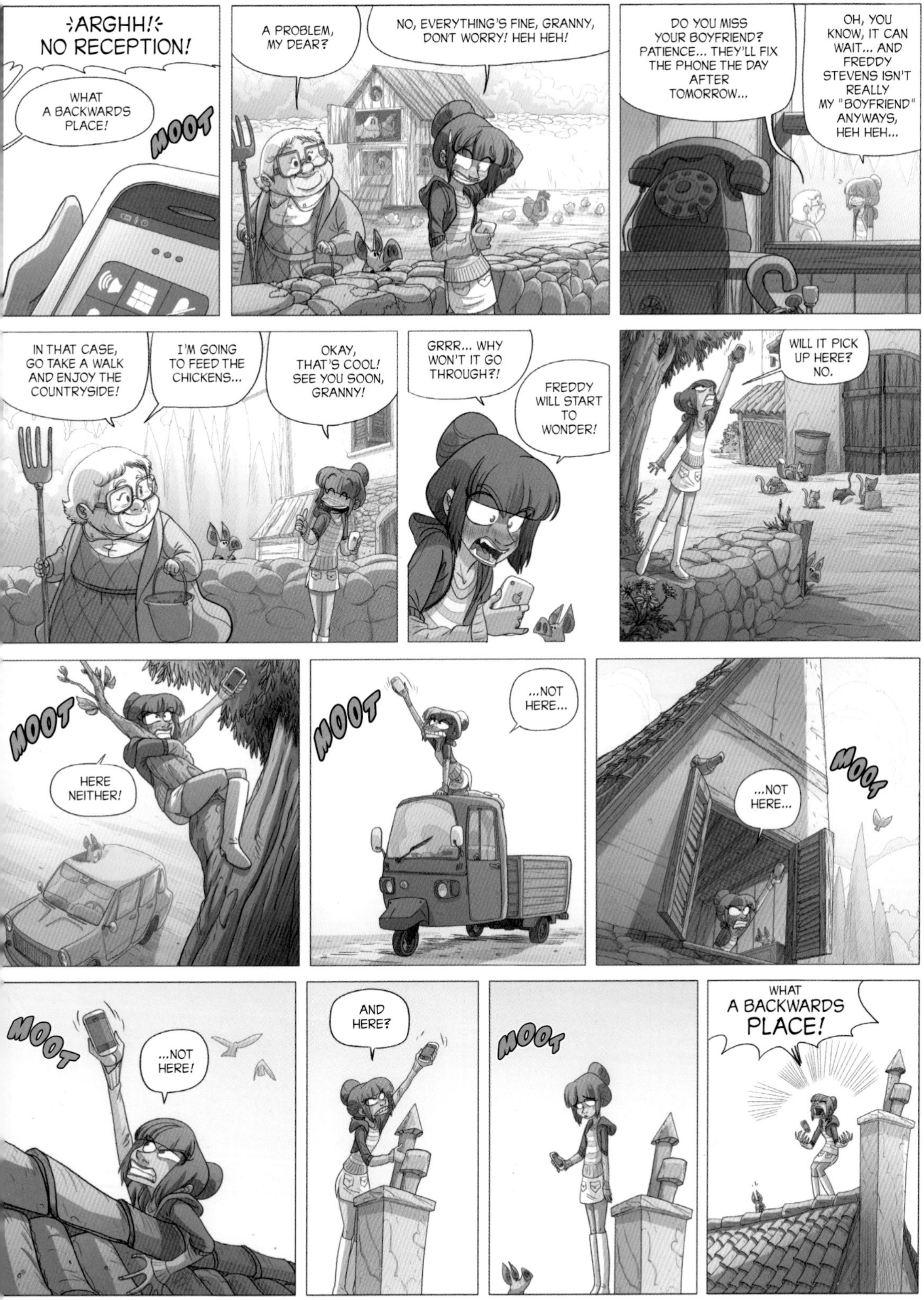

ARGHH! NO RECEPTION!
WHAT A BACKWARDS PLACE!
MOOT
A PROBLEM, MY DEAR?
NO, EVERYTHING'S FINE, GRANNY, DON'T WORRY! HEH HEH!
DO YOU MISS YOUR BOYFRIEND? PATIENCE... THEY'LL FIX THE PHONE THE DAY AFTER TOMORROW...
OH, YOU KNOW, IT CAN WAIT... AND FREDDY STEVENS ISN'T REALLY MY "BOYFRIEND" ANYWAYS, HEH HEH...
IN THAT CASE, GO TAKE A WALK AND ENJOY THE COUNTRYSIDE!
I'M GOING TO FEED THE CHICKENS...
OKAY, THAT'S COOL! SEE YOU SOON, GRANNY!
GRRR... WHY WON'T IT GO THROUGH?!
FREDDY WILL START TO WONDER!
WILL IT PICK UP HERE? NO.
MOOT
HERE NEITHER!
MOOT
...NOT HERE...
MOOT
...NOT HERE...
MOOT
...NOT HERE!
AND HERE?
MOOT
WHAT A BACKWARDS PLACE!

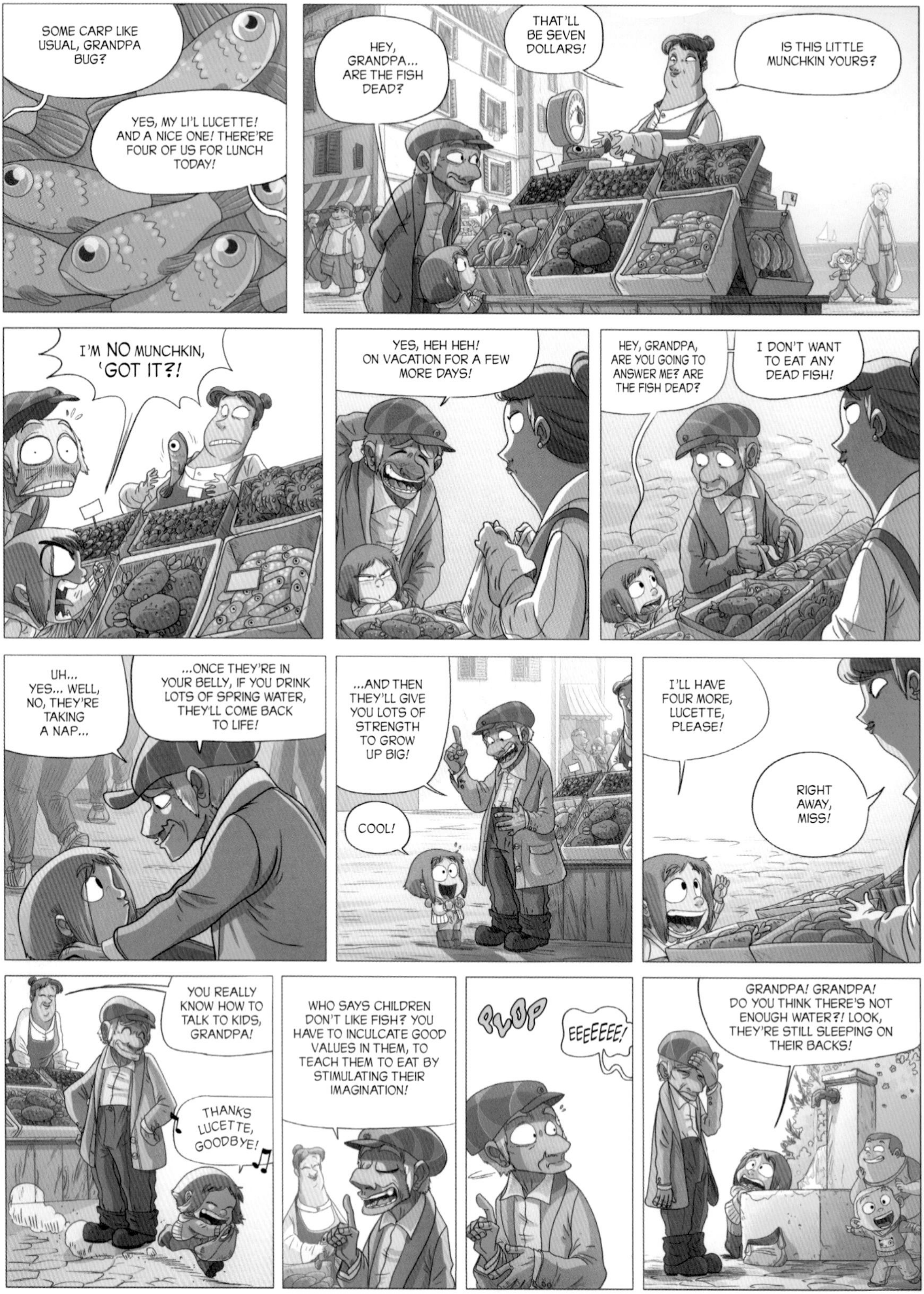
SOME CARP LIKE USUAL, GRANDPA BUG?
YES, MY LI'L LUCETTE! AND A NICE ONE! THERE'RE FOUR OF US FOR LUNCH TODAY!
HEY, GRANDPA... ARE THE FISH DEAD?
THAT'LL BE SEVEN DOLLARS!
IS THIS LITTLE MUNCHKIN YOURS?
I'M NO MUNCHKIN, 'GOT IT?!
YES, HEH HEH! ON VACATION FOR A FEW MORE DAYS!
HEY, GRANDPA, ARE YOU GOING TO ANSWER ME? ARE THE FISH DEAD?
I DON'T WANT TO EAT ANY DEAD FISH!
UH... YES... WELL, NO, THEY'RE TAKING A NAP...
...ONCE THEY'RE IN YOUR BELLY, IF YOU DRINK LOTS OF SPRING WATER, THEY'LL COME BACK TO LIFE!
...AND THEN THEY'LL GIVE YOU LOTS OF STRENGTH TO GROW UP BIG!
COOL!
I'LL HAVE FOUR MORE, LUCETTE, PLEASE!
RIGHT AWAY, MISS!
YOU REALLY KNOW HOW TO TALK TO KIDS, GRANDPA!
THANKS LUCETTE, GOODBYE!
WHO SAYS CHILDREN DON'T LIKE FISH? YOU HAVE TO INCULCATE GOOD VALUES IN THEM, TO TEACH THEM TO EAT BY STIMULATING THEIR IMAGINATION!
PLOP
EEEEEEE!
GRANDPA! GRANDPA! DO YOU THINK THERE'S NOT ENOUGH WATER?! LOOK, THEY'RE STILL SLEEPING ON THEIR BACKS!

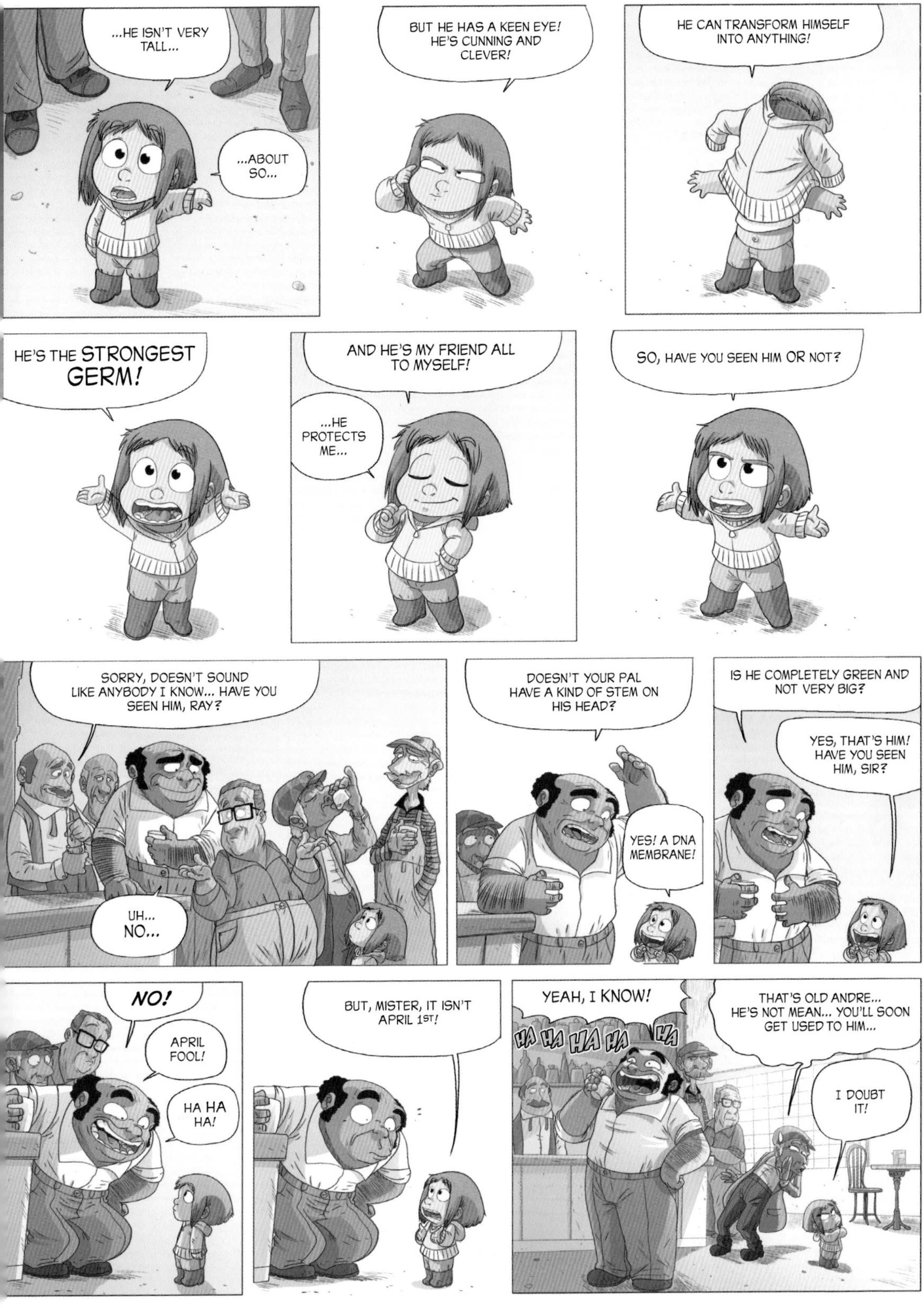
...HE ISN'T VERY TALL...
...ABOUT SO...
BUT HE HAS A KEEN EYE! HE'S CUNNING AND CLEVER!
HE CAN TRANSFORM HIMSELF INTO ANYTHING!
HE'S THE STRONGEST GERM!
AND HE'S MY FRIEND ALL TO MYSELF!
...HE PROTECTS ME...
SO, HAVE YOU SEEN HIM OR NOT?
SORRY, DOESN'T SOUND LIKE ANYBODY I KNOW... HAVE YOU SEEN HIM, RAY?
UH... NO...
DOESN'T YOUR PAL HAVE A KIND OF STEM ON HIS HEAD?
YES! A DNA MEMBRANE!
IS HE COMPLETELY GREEN AND NOT VERY BIG?
YES, THAT'S HIM! HAVE YOU SEEN HIM, SIR?
NO!
APRIL FOOL!
HA HA HA!
BUT, MISTER, IT ISN'T APRIL 1ST!
YEAH, I KNOW!
HA HA HA HA HA
THAT'S OLD ANDRE... HE'S NOT MEAN... YOU'LL SOON GET USED TO HIM...
I DOUBT IT!

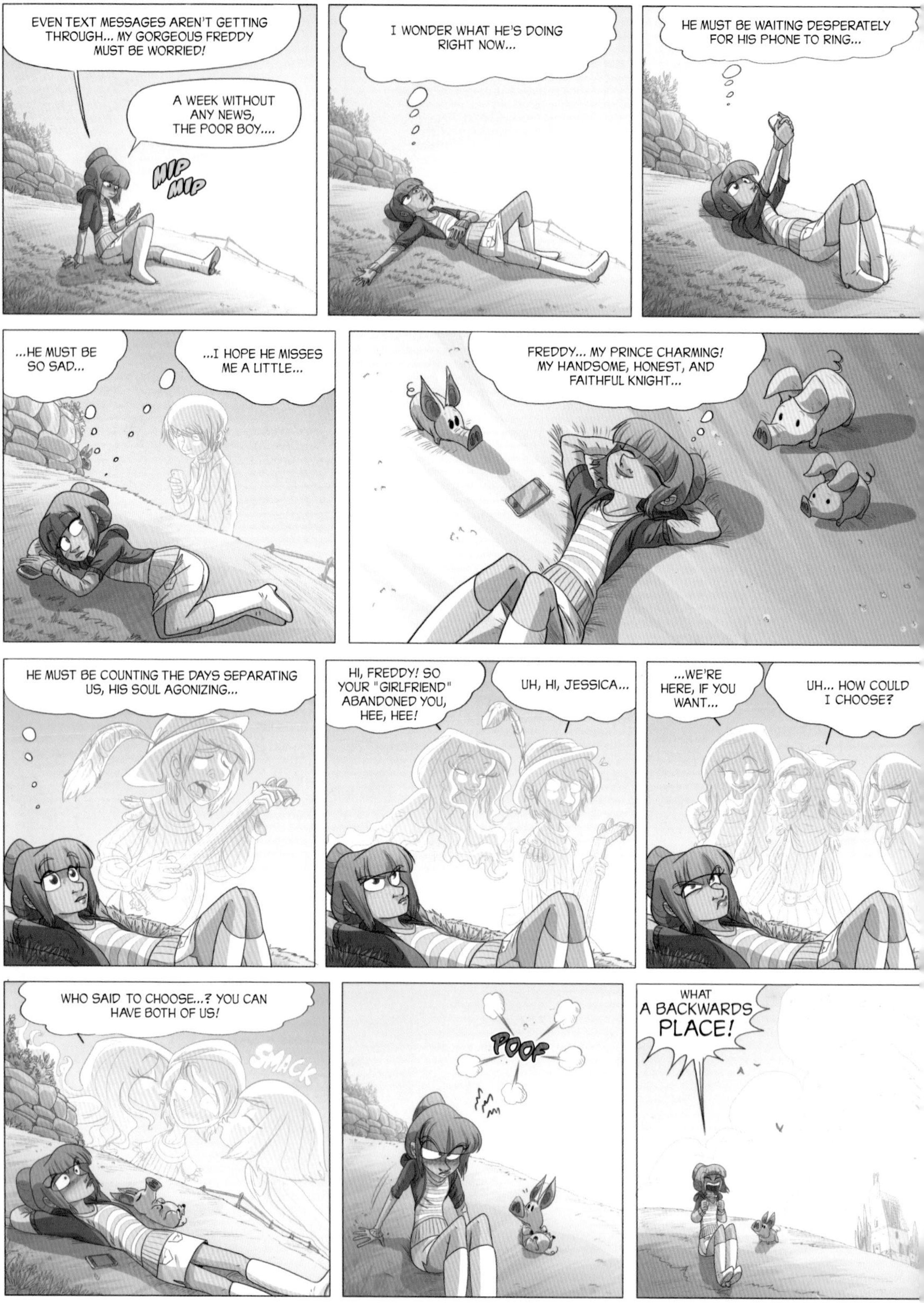
EVEN TEXT MESSAGES AREN'T GETTING THROUGH... MY GORGEOUS FREDDY MUST BE WORRIED!
A WEEK WITHOUT ANY NEWS, THE POOR BOY....
MIP MIP
I WONDER WHAT HE'S DOING RIGHT NOW...
HE MUST BE WAITING DESPERATELY FOR HIS PHONE TO RING...
...HE MUST BE SO SAD...
...I HOPE HE MISSES ME A LITTLE...
FREDDY... MY PRINCE CHARMING! MY HANDSOME, HONEST, AND FAITHFUL KNIGHT...
HE MUST BE COUNTING THE DAYS SEPARATING US, HIS SOUL AGONIZING...
HI, FREDDY! SO YOUR "GIRLFRIEND" ABANDONED YOU, HEE, HEE!
UH, HI, JESSICA...
...WE'RE HERE, IF YOU WANT...
UH... HOW COULD I CHOOSE?
WHO SAID TO CHOOSE...? YOU CAN HAVE BOTH OF US!
SMACK
POOF
WHAT A BACKWARDS PLACE!

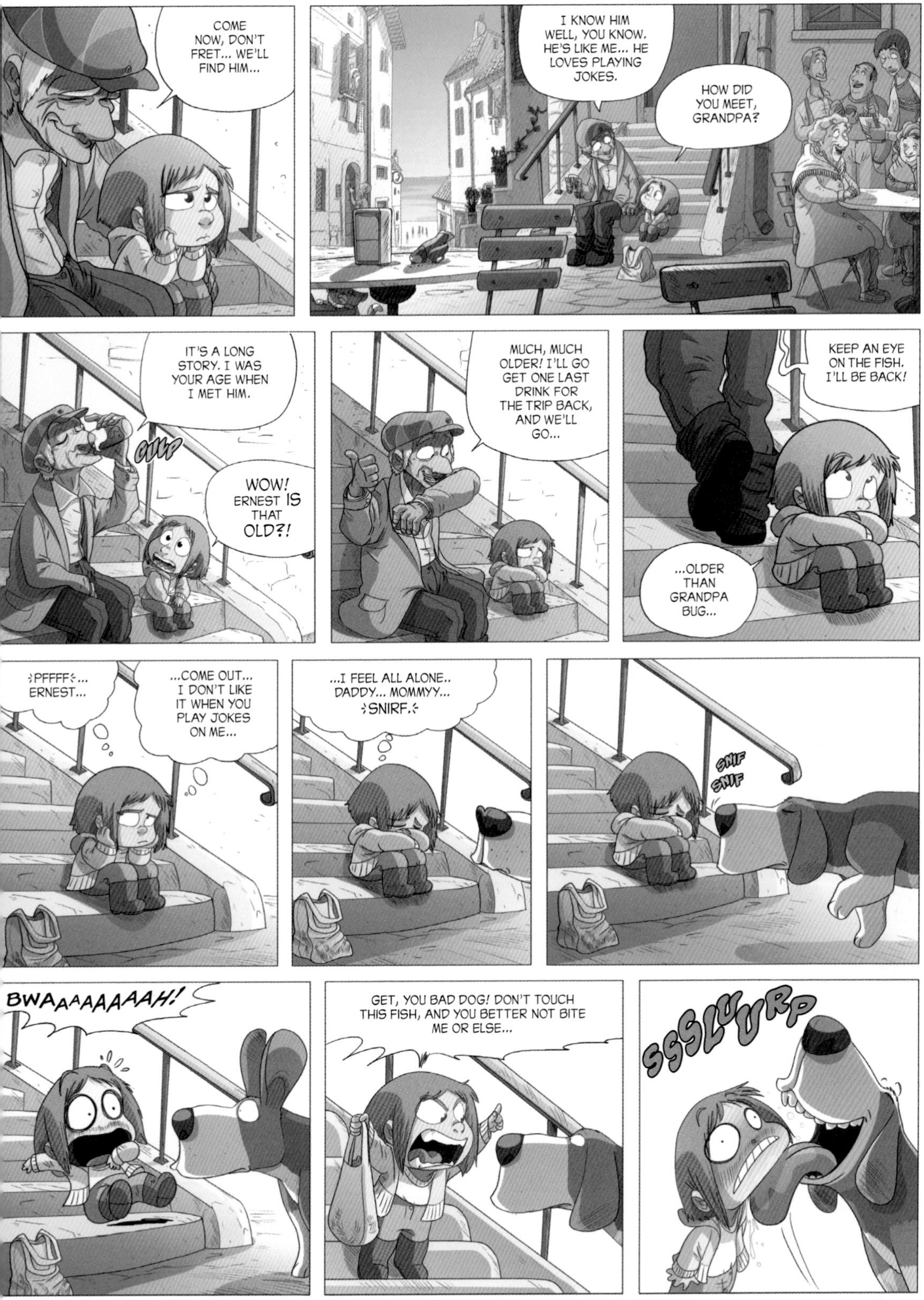
COME NOW, DON'T FRET... WE'LL FIND HIM...
I KNOW HIM WELL, YOU KNOW. HE'S LIKE ME... HE LOVES PLAYING JOKES.
HOW DID YOU MEET, GRANDPA?
IT'S A LONG STORY. I WAS YOUR AGE WHEN I MET HIM.
GULP
WOW! ERNEST IS THAT OLD?!
MUCH, MUCH OLDER! I'LL GO GET ONE LAST DRINK FOR THE TRIP BACK, AND WE'LL GO...
KEEP AN EYE ON THE FISH. I'LL BE BACK!
...OLDER THAN GRANDPA BUG...
PFFFF... ERNEST...
...COME OUT... I DON'T LIKE IT WHEN YOU PLAY JOKES ON ME...
...I FEEL ALL ALONE.. DADDY... MOMMYY... SNIRF.
SNIF
SNIF
BWAAAAAAAAH!
GET, YOU BAD DOG! DON'T TOUCH THIS FISH, AND YOU BETTER NOT BITE ME OR ELSE...
SSSLUURP

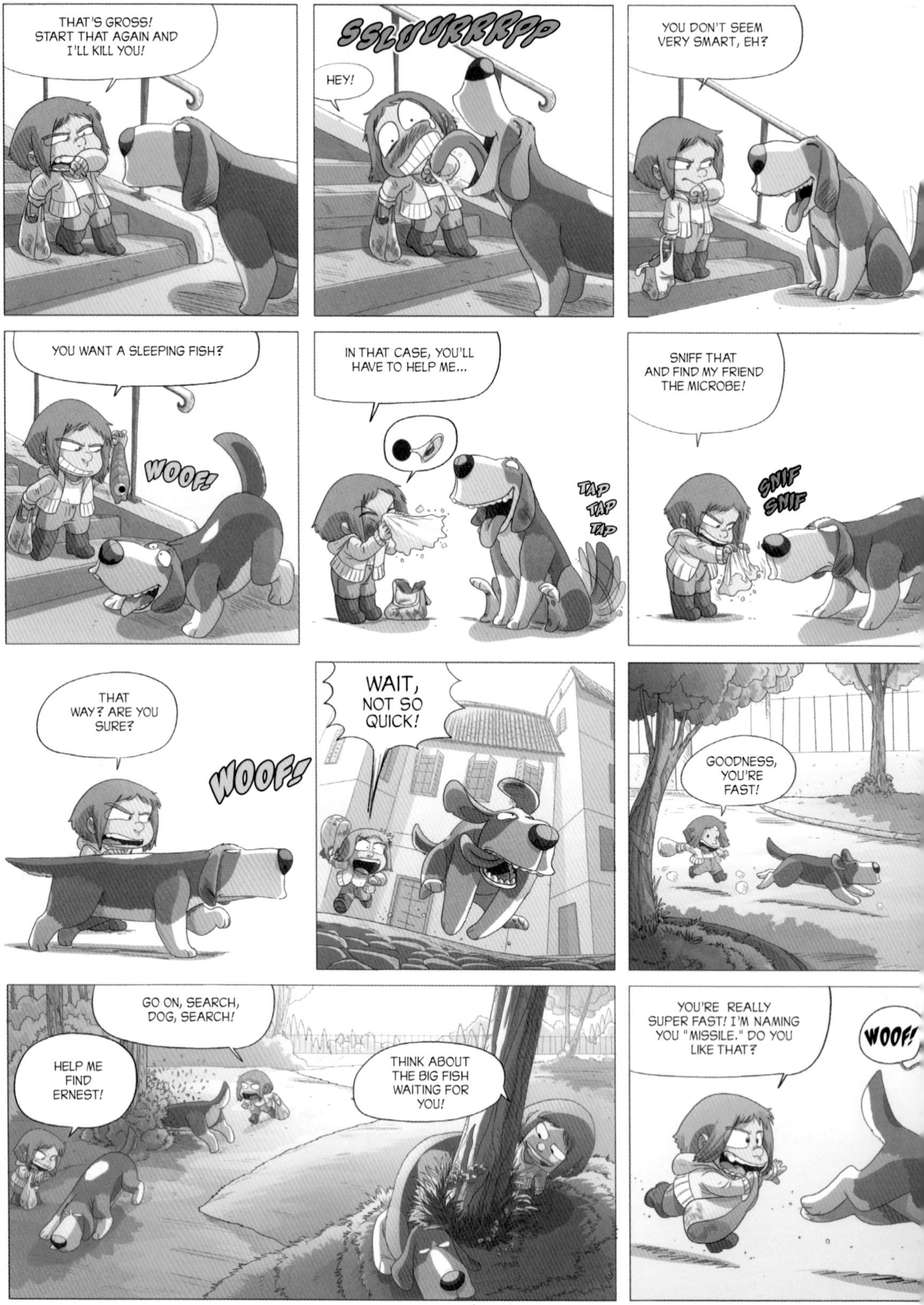
THAT'S GROSS! START THAT AGAIN AND I'LL KILL YOU!
SSLUURRRPP
HEY!
YOU DON'T SEEM VERY SMART, EH?
YOU WANT A SLEEPING FISH?
WOOF!
IN THAT CASE, YOU'LL HAVE TO HELP ME...
TAP TAP TAP
SNIFF THAT AND FIND MY FRIEND THE MICROBE!
SNIF SNIF
THAT WAY? ARE YOU SURE?
WOOF!
WAIT, NOT SO QUICK!
GOODNESS, YOU'RE FAST!
GO ON, SEARCH, DOG, SEARCH!
HELP ME FIND ERNEST!
THINK ABOUT THE BIG FISH WAITING FOR YOU!
YOU'RE REALLY SUPER FAST! I'M NAMING YOU "MISSILE." DO YOU LIKE THAT?
WOOF!

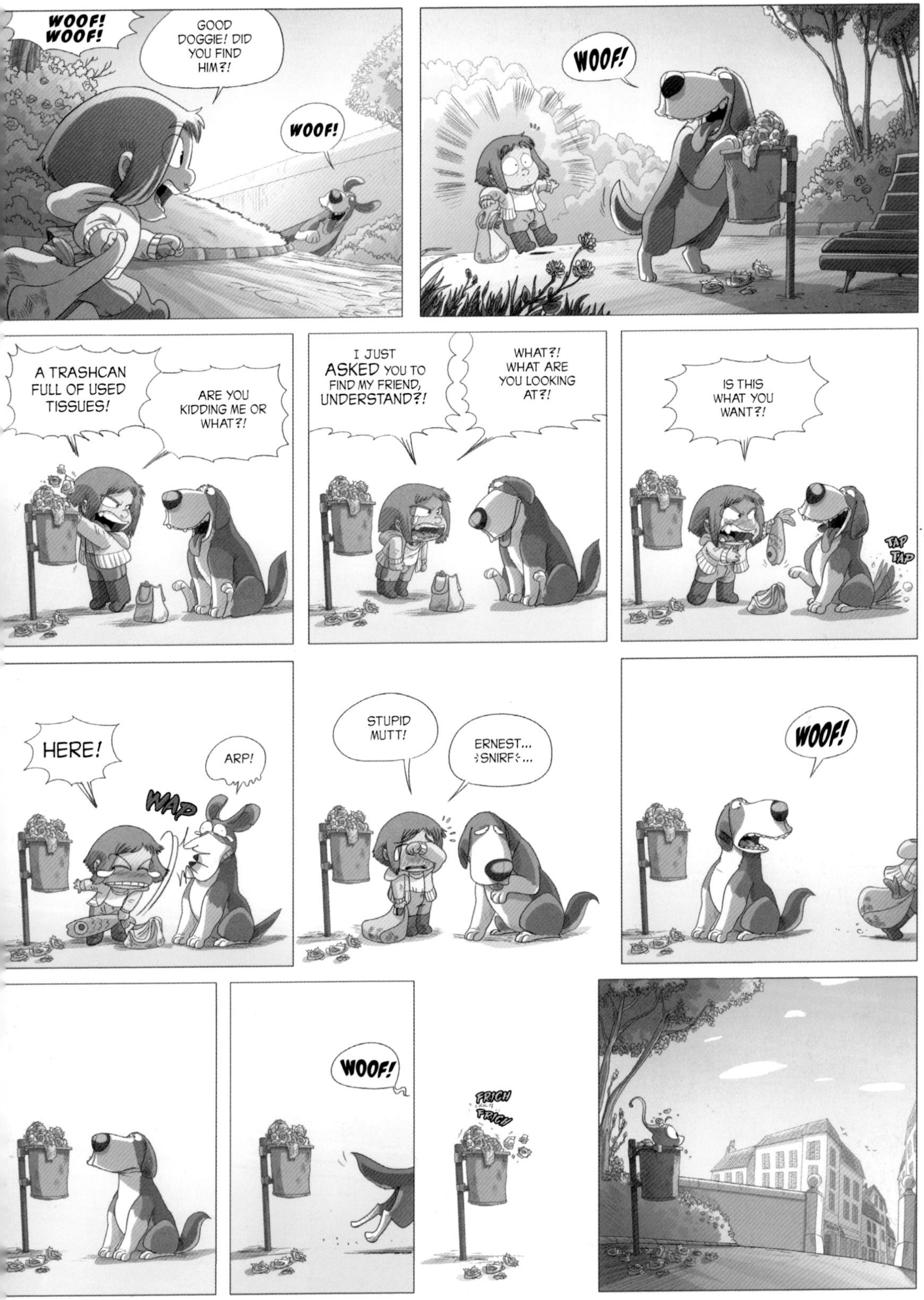
WOOF! WOOF!
GOOD DOGGIE! DID YOU FIND HIM?!
WOOF!
WOOF!
A TRASHCAN FULL OF USED TISSUES!
ARE YOU KIDDING ME OR WHAT?!
I JUST ASKED YOU TO FIND MY FRIEND, UNDERSTAND?!
WHAT?! WHAT ARE YOU LOOKING AT?!
IS THIS WHAT YOU WANT?!
TAP TAP
HERE!
WAP
ARP!
STUPID MUTT!
ERNEST... SNIRF...
WOOF!
WOOF!
FRICH FRICH

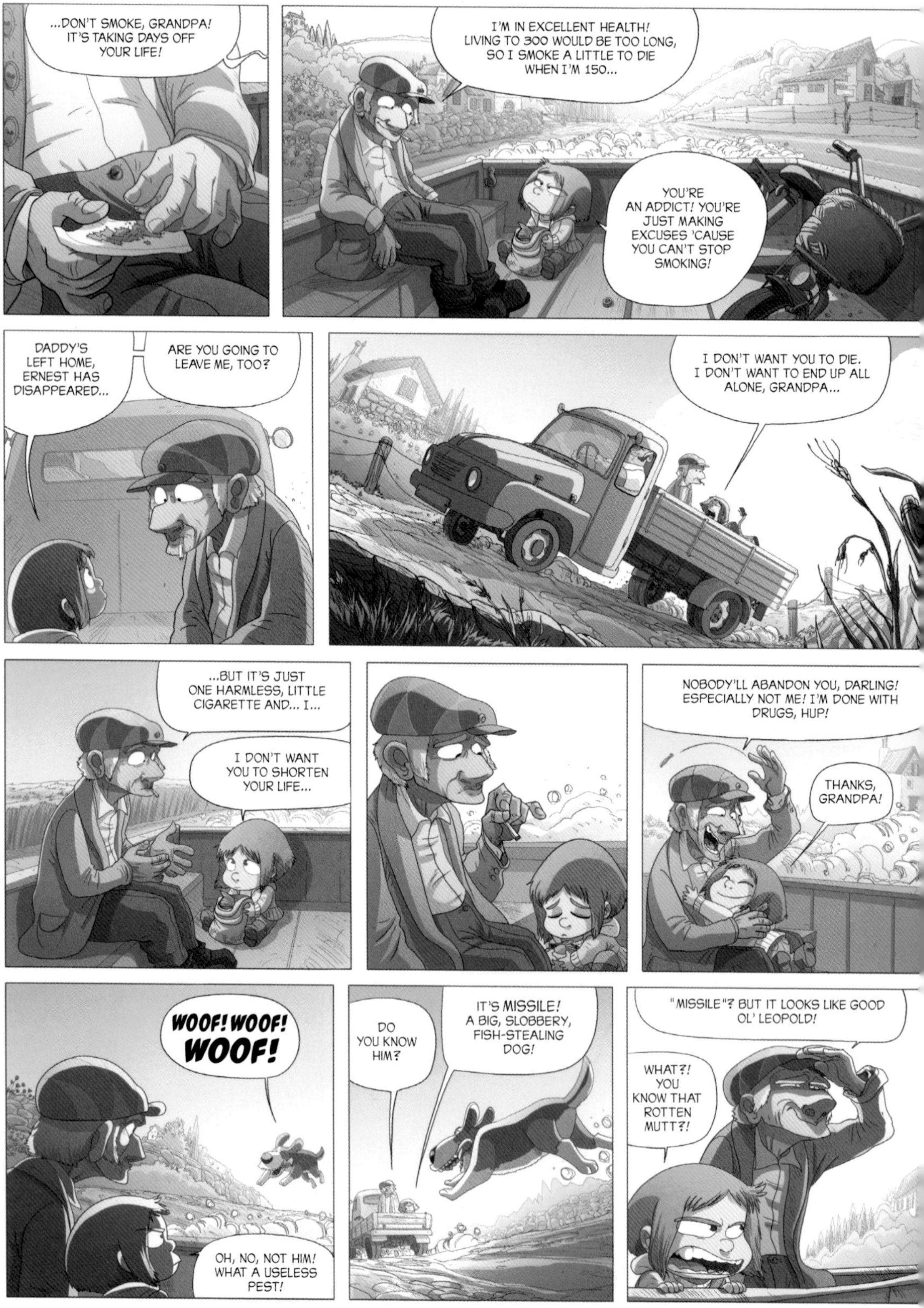
...DON'T SMOKE, GRANDPA! IT'S TAKING DAYS OFF YOUR LIFE!
I'M IN EXCELLENT HEALTH! LIVING TO 300 WOULD BE TOO LONG, SO I SMOKE A LITTLE TO DIE WHEN I'M 150...
YOU'RE AN ADDICT! YOU'RE JUST MAKING EXCUSES 'CAUSE YOU CAN'T STOP SMOKING!
DADDY'S LEFT HOME, ERNEST HAS DISAPPEARED...
ARE YOU GOING TO LEAVE ME, TOO?
I DON'T WANT YOU TO DIE. I DON'T WANT TO END UP ALL ALONE, GRANDPA...
...BUT IT'S JUST ONE HARMLESS, LITTLE CIGARETTE AND... I...
I DON'T WANT YOU TO SHORTEN YOUR LIFE...
NOBODY'LL ABANDON YOU, DARLING! ESPECIALLY NOT ME! I'M DONE WITH DRUGS, HUP!
THANKS, GRANDPA!
WOOF! WOOF! WOOF!
OH, NO, NOT HIM! WHAT A USELESS PEST!
DO YOU KNOW HIM?
IT'S MISSILE! A BIG, SLOBBERY, FISH-STEALING DOG!
"MISSILE"? BUT IT LOOKS LIKE GOOD OL' LEOPOLD!
WHAT?! YOU KNOW THAT ROTTEN MUTT?!

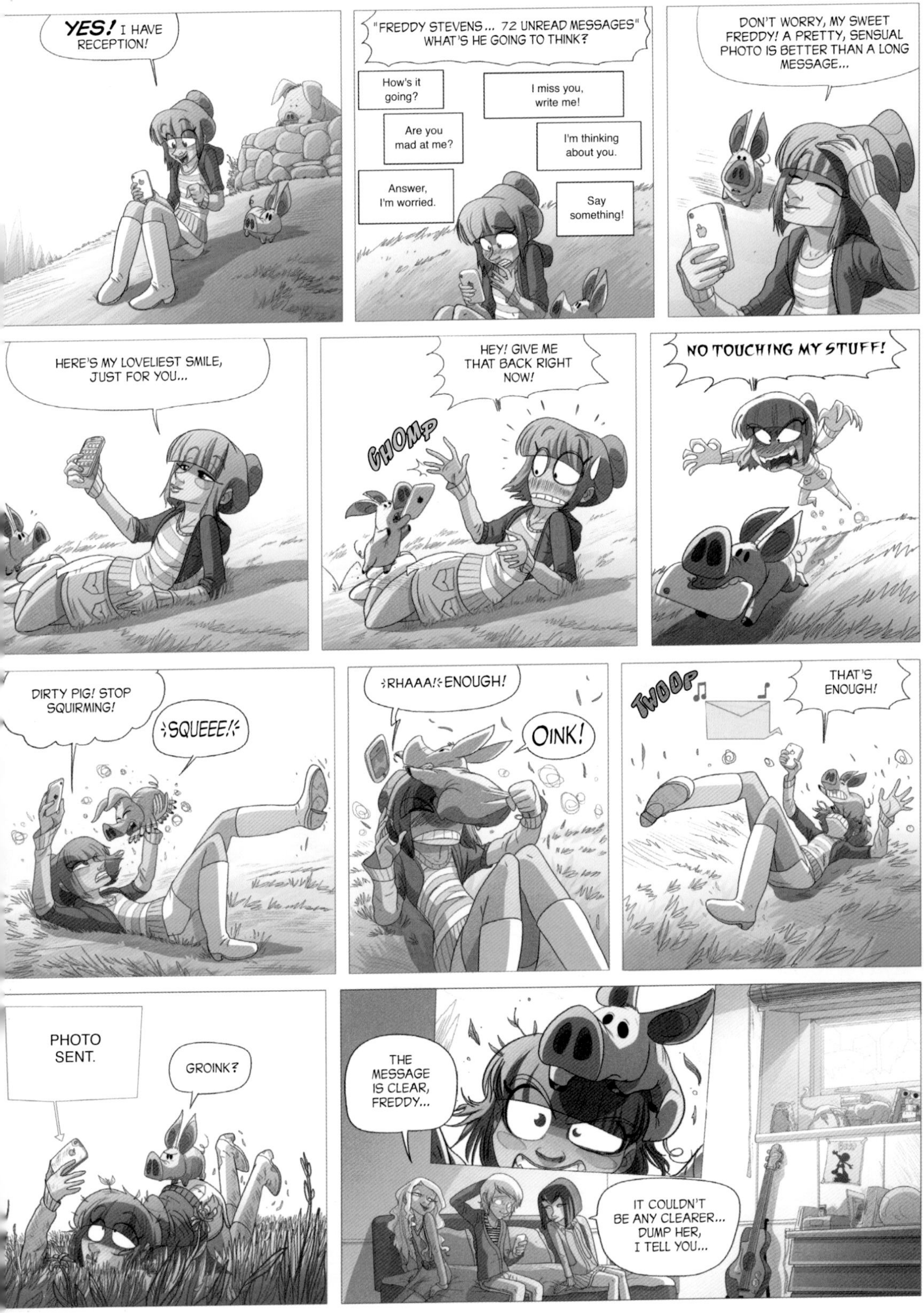
YES! I HAVE RECEPTION!
"FREDDY STEVENS... 72 UNREAD MESSAGES" WHAT'S HE GOING TO THINK?
How's it going?
I miss you, write me!
Are you mad at me?
I'm thinking about you.
Answer, I'm worried.
Say something!
DON'T WORRY, MY SWEET FREDDY! A PRETTY, SENSUAL PHOTO IS BETTER THAN A LONG MESSAGE...
HERE'S MY LOVELIEST SMILE, JUST FOR YOU...
HEY! GIVE ME THAT BACK RIGHT NOW!
CHOMP
NO TOUCHING MY STUFF!
DIRTY PIG! STOP SQUIRMING!
SQUEEE!
RHAAA! ENOUGH!
OINK!
TWOOP
THAT'S ENOUGH!
PHOTO SENT.
GROINK?
THE MESSAGE IS CLEAR, FREDDY...
IT COULDN'T BE ANY CLEARER... DUMP HER, I TELL YOU...

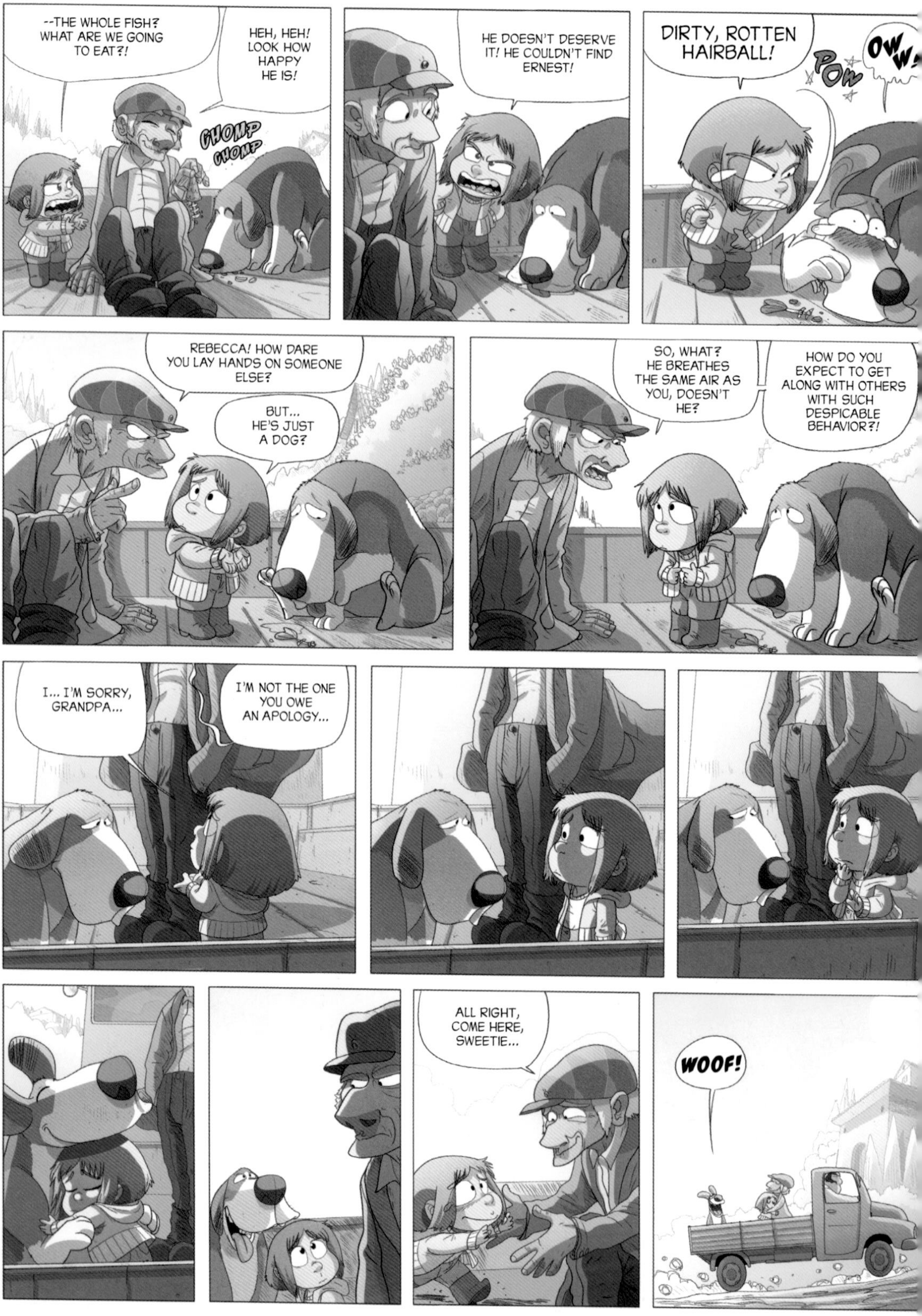
--THE WHOLE FISH? WHAT ARE WE GOING TO EAT?!
HEH, HEH! LOOK HOW HAPPY HE IS!
CHOMP CHOMP
HE DOESN'T DESERVE IT! HE COULDN'T FIND ERNEST!
DIRTY, ROTTEN HAIRBALL!
POW
OWW!
REBECCA! HOW DARE YOU LAY HANDS ON SOMEONE ELSE?
BUT... HE'S JUST A DOG?
SO, WHAT? HE BREATHES THE SAME AIR AS YOU, DOESN'T HE?
HOW DO YOU EXPECT TO GET ALONG WITH OTHERS WITH SUCH DESPICABLE BEHAVIOR?!
I... I'M SORRY, GRANDPA...
I'M NOT THE ONE YOU OWE AN APOLOGY...
ALL RIGHT, COME HERE, SWEETIE...
WOOF!

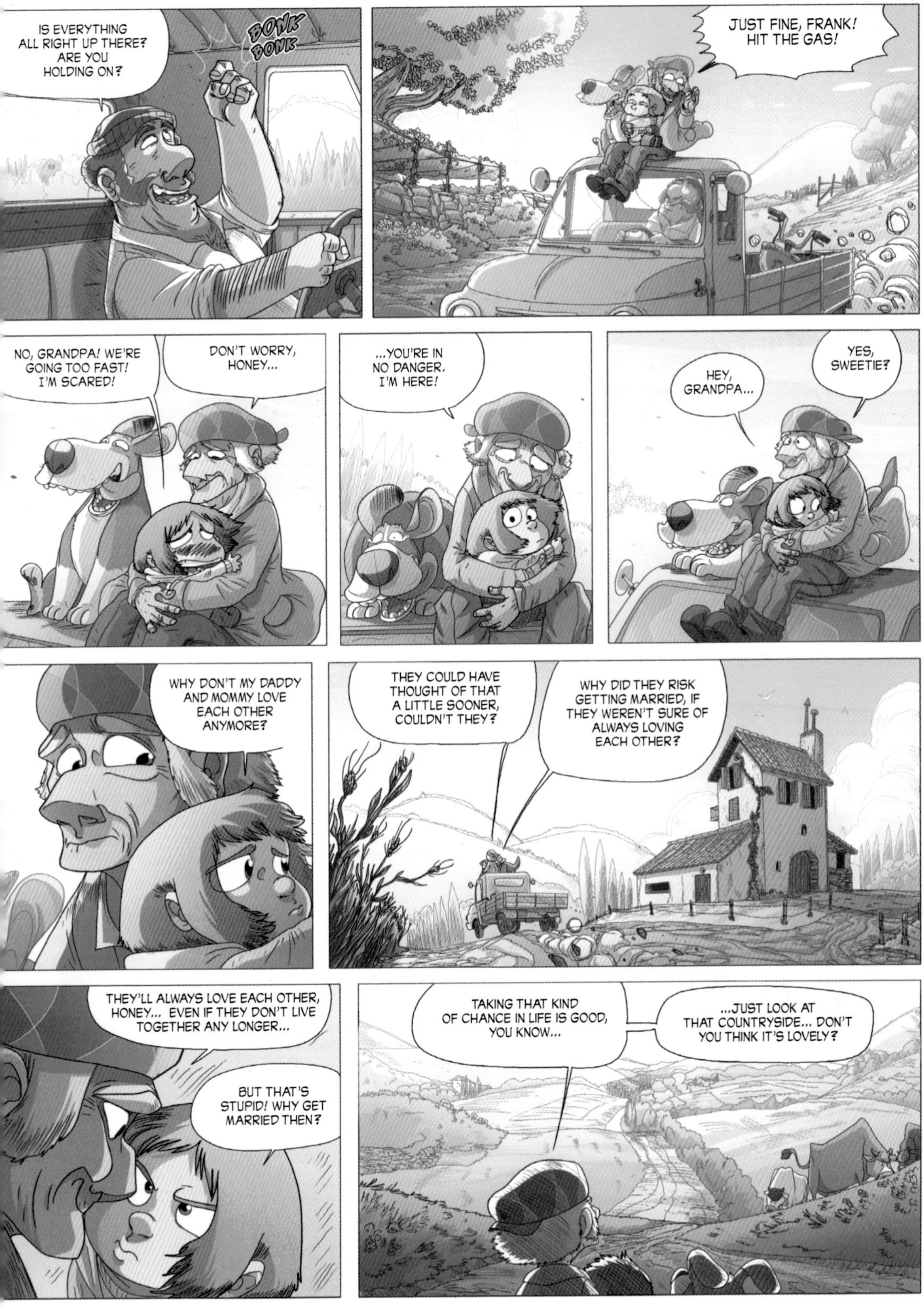
IS EVERYTHING ALL RIGHT UP THERE? ARE YOU HOLDING ON?
BONK BONK
JUST FINE, FRANK! HIT THE GAS!
NO, GRANDPA! WE'RE GOING TOO FAST! I'M SCARED!
DON'T WORRY, HONEY...
...YOU'RE IN NO DANGER. I'M HERE!
HEY, GRANDPA...
YES, SWEETIE?
WHY DON'T MY DADDY AND MOMMY LOVE EACH OTHER ANYMORE?
THEY COULD HAVE THOUGHT OF THAT A LITTLE SOONER, COULDN'T THEY?
WHY DID THEY RISK GETTING MARRIED, IF THEY WEREN'T SURE OF ALWAYS LOVING EACH OTHER?
THEY'LL ALWAYS LOVE EACH OTHER, HONEY... EVEN IF THEY DON'T LIVE TOGETHER ANY LONGER...
BUT THAT'S STUPID! WHY GET MARRIED THEN?
TAKING THAT KIND OF CHANCE IN LIFE IS GOOD, YOU KNOW...
...JUST LOOK AT THAT COUNTRYSIDE... DON'T YOU THINK IT'S LOVELY?

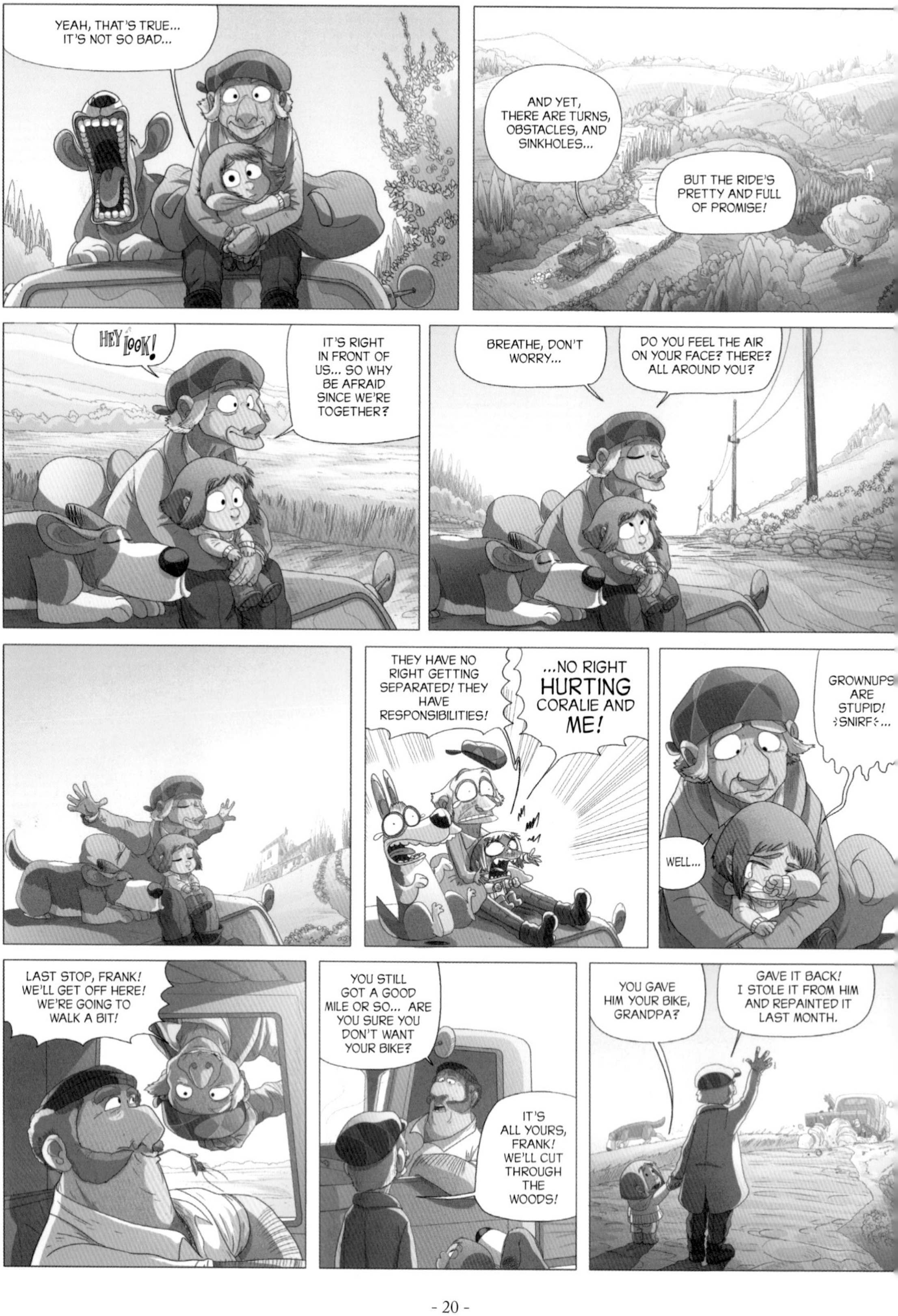
YEAH, THAT'S TRUE... IT'S NOT SO BAD...
AND YET, THERE ARE TURNS, OBSTACLES, AND SINKHOLES...
BUT THE RIDE'S PRETTY AND FULL OF PROMISE!
HEY LOOK!
IT'S RIGHT IN FRONT OF US... SO WHY BE AFRAID SINCE WE'RE TOGETHER?
BREATHE, DON'T WORRY...
DO YOU FEEL THE AIR ON YOUR FACE? THERE? ALL AROUND YOU?
THEY HAVE NO RIGHT GETTING SEPARATED! THEY HAVE RESPONSIBILITIES!
...NO RIGHT HURTING CORALIE AND ME!
GROWNUPS ARE STUPID! SNIRF...
WELL...
LAST STOP, FRANK! WE'LL GET OFF HERE! WE'RE GOING TO WALK A BIT!
YOU STILL GOT A GOOD MILE OR SO... ARE YOU SURE YOU DON'T WANT YOUR BIKE?
IT'S ALL YOURS, FRANK! WE'LL CUT THROUGH THE WOODS!
YOU GAVE HIM YOUR BIKE, GRANDPA?
GAVE IT BACK! I STOLE IT FROM HIM AND REPAINTED IT LAST MONTH.

IT'S NICE HAVING A GRANDPA... IT'S MAGICAL! IT'S A LITTLE LIKE HAVING A MICROBE FRIEND. HE KNOWS LOTS OF STUFF THAT'S GOOD FOR YOU...

WE GATHERED SOME THYME TO MAKE HERBAL TEAS FOR INDIGESTION AND LOTION FOR DANDRUFF IN YOUR HAIR...

WE ALSO FOUND SOME LETTUCE AND WILD PARSLEY... IT'S LESS EXPENSIVE THAN IN THE STORE AND TASTES BETTER... (BUT IT'S FULL OF DIRT...)

THEN WE CROSSED A BIG FIELD OF LAVENDER. IT SMELLED SO GOOD...!

WE MADE A PRETTY BOUQUET SO GRANNY DOODLE CAN SCENT HER LINENS...

I TASTED MY FIRST CHERRIES... THEY WEREN'T QUITE RIPE, BUT THEY WERE DELICIOUS!

WE EACH MADE A WISH... (I'M NOT ALLOWED TO SAY MINE, OTHERWISE IT WON'T COME TRUE...)

GRANDPA TOLD ME I WAS HIS "LITTLE PRINCESS OF THE FOREST," AND HE GAVE ME SOME PRETTY EARRINGS...

GRANDPA IS THE ONLY PERSON I KNOW WHO DOESN'T LIKE TV... HE THINKS IT'S DEAFENING.

"NATURE OFFERS A LOT MORE DAZZLING SIGHTS FOR SOMEONE WHO CAN BE QUIET AND LISTEN..." MY GRANDPA'S WEIRD...

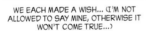

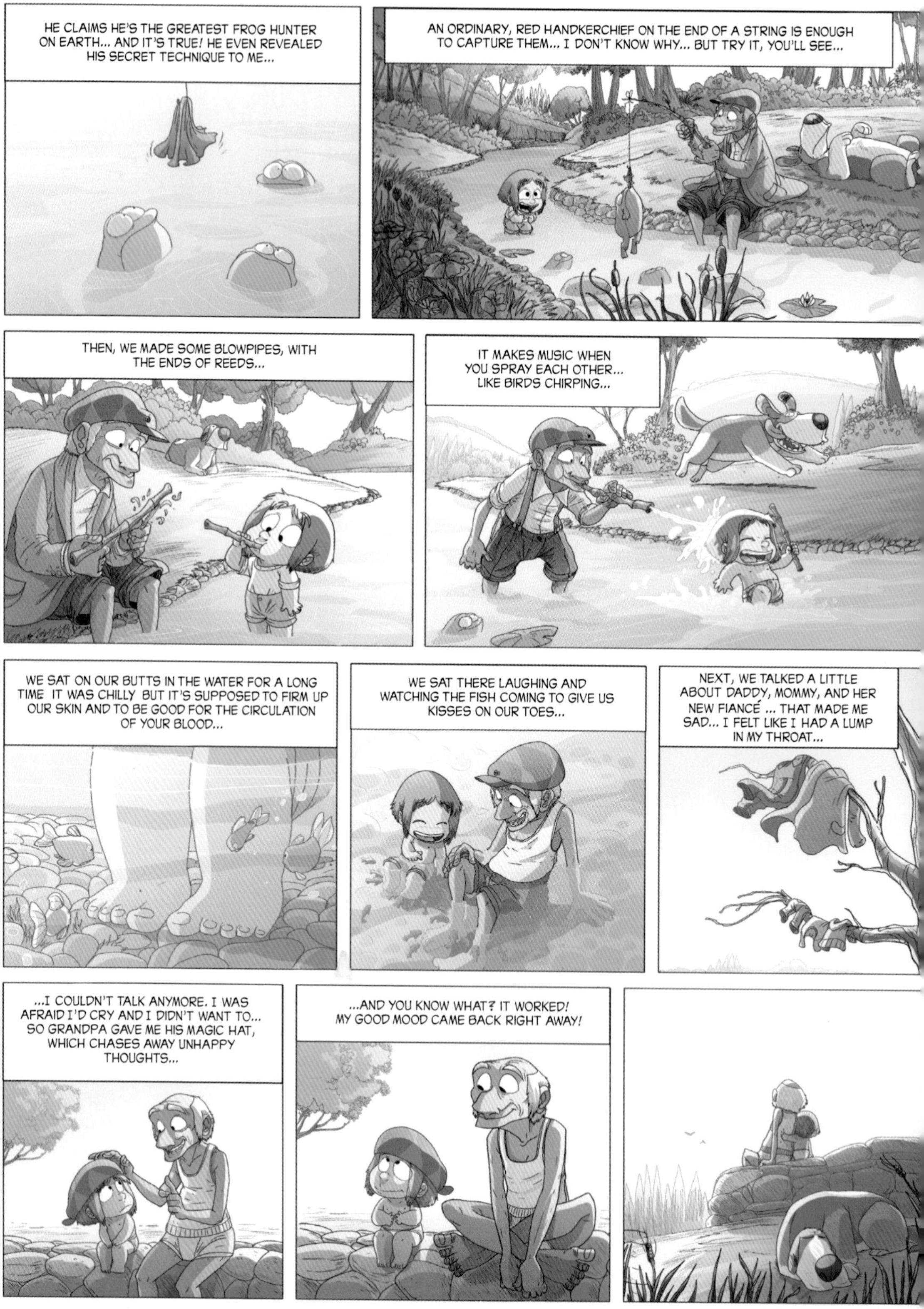
HE CLAIMS HE'S THE GREATEST FROG HUNTER ON EARTH... AND IT'S TRUE! HE EVEN REVEALED HIS SECRET TECHNIQUE TO ME...
AN ORDINARY, RED HANDKERCHIEF ON THE END OF A STRING IS ENOUGH TO CAPTURE THEM... I DON'T KNOW WHY... BUT TRY IT, YOU'LL SEE...
THEN, WE MADE SOME BLOWPIPES, WITH THE ENDS OF REEDS...
IT MAKES MUSIC WHEN YOU SPRAY EACH OTHER... LIKE BIRDS CHIRPING...
WE SAT ON OUR BUTTS IN THE WATER FOR A LONG TIME IT WAS CHILLY BUT IT'S SUPPOSED TO FIRM UP OUR SKIN AND TO BE GOOD FOR THE CIRCULATION OF YOUR BLOOD...
WE SAT THERE LAUGHING AND WATCHING THE FISH COMING TO GIVE US KISSES ON OUR TOES...
NEXT, WE TALKED A LITTLE ABOUT DADDY, MOMMY, AND HER NEW FIANCÉ ... THAT MADE ME SAD... I FELT LIKE I HAD A LUMP IN MY THROAT...
...I COULDN'T TALK ANYMORE. I WAS AFRAID I'D CRY AND I DIDN'T WANT TO... SO GRANDPA GAVE ME HIS MAGIC HAT, WHICH CHASES AWAY UNHAPPY THOUGHTS...
...AND YOU KNOW WHAT? IT WORKED! MY GOOD MOOD CAME BACK RIGHT AWAY!

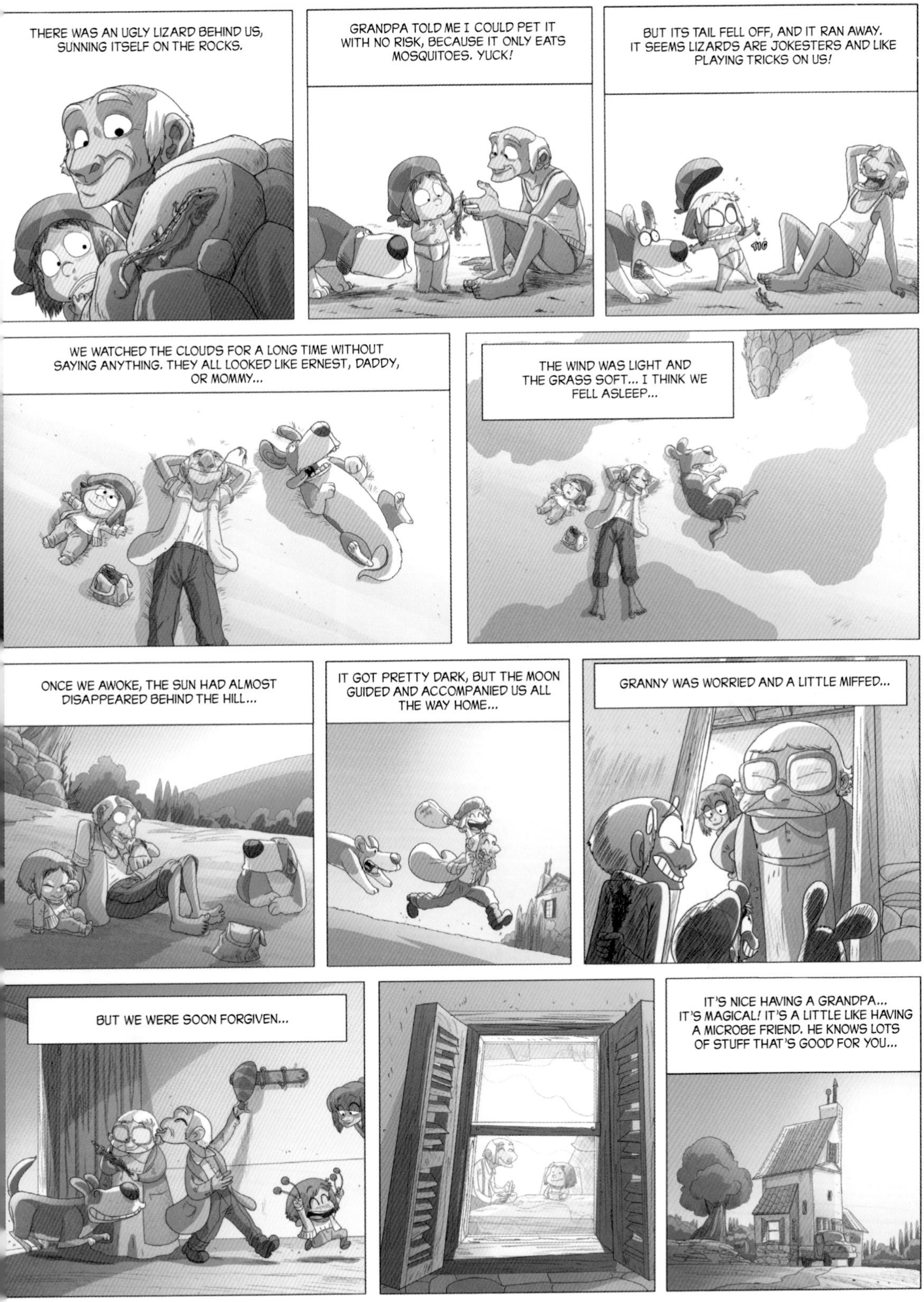
THERE WAS AN UGLY LIZARD BEHIND US, SUNNING ITSELF ON THE ROCKS.
GRANDPA TOLD ME I COULD PET IT WITH NO RISK, BECAUSE IT ONLY EATS MOSQUITOES. YUCK!
BUT ITS TAIL FELL OFF, AND IT RAN AWAY. IT SEEMS LIZARDS ARE JOKESTERS AND LIKE PLAYING TRICKS ON US!
TIC
WE WATCHED THE CLOUDS FOR A LONG TIME WITHOUT SAYING ANYTHING. THEY ALL LOOKED LIKE ERNEST, DADDY, OR MOMMY...
THE WIND WAS LIGHT AND THE GRASS SOFT... I THINK WE FELL ASLEEP...
ONCE WE AWOKE, THE SUN HAD ALMOST DISAPPEARED BEHIND THE HILL...
IT GOT PRETTY DARK, BUT THE MOON GUIDED AND ACCOMPANIED US ALL THE WAY HOME...
GRANNY WAS WORRIED AND A LITTLE MIFFED...
BUT WE WERE SOON FORGIVEN...
IT'S NICE HAVING A GRANDPA... IT'S MAGICAL! IT'S A LITTLE LIKE HAVING A MICROBE FRIEND. HE KNOWS LOTS OF STUFF THAT'S GOOD FOR YOU...

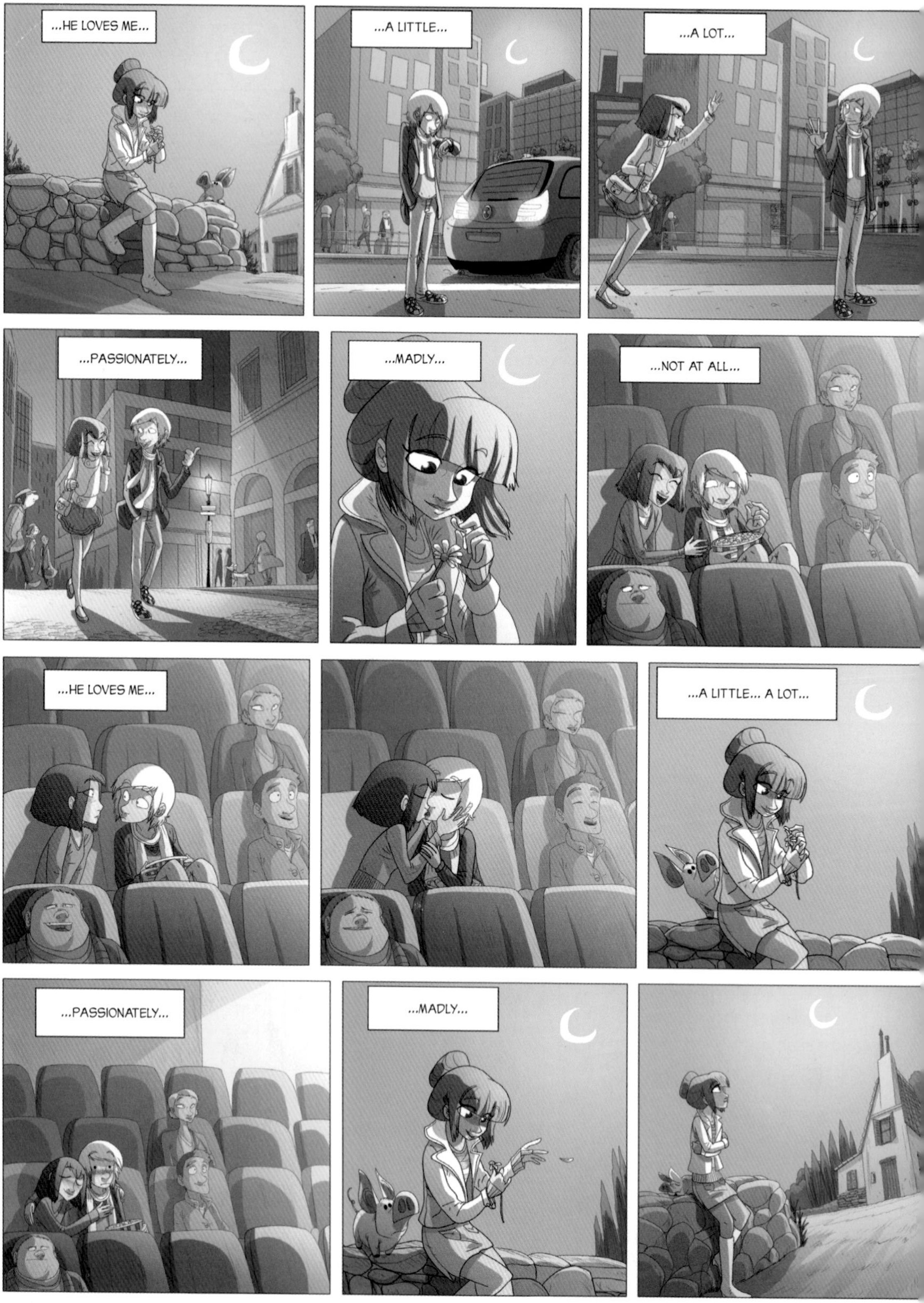
...HE LOVES ME...
...A LITTLE...
...A LOT...
...PASSIONATELY...
...MADLY...
...NOT AT ALL...
...HE LOVES ME...
...A LITTLE... A LOT...
...PASSIONATELY...
...MADLY...

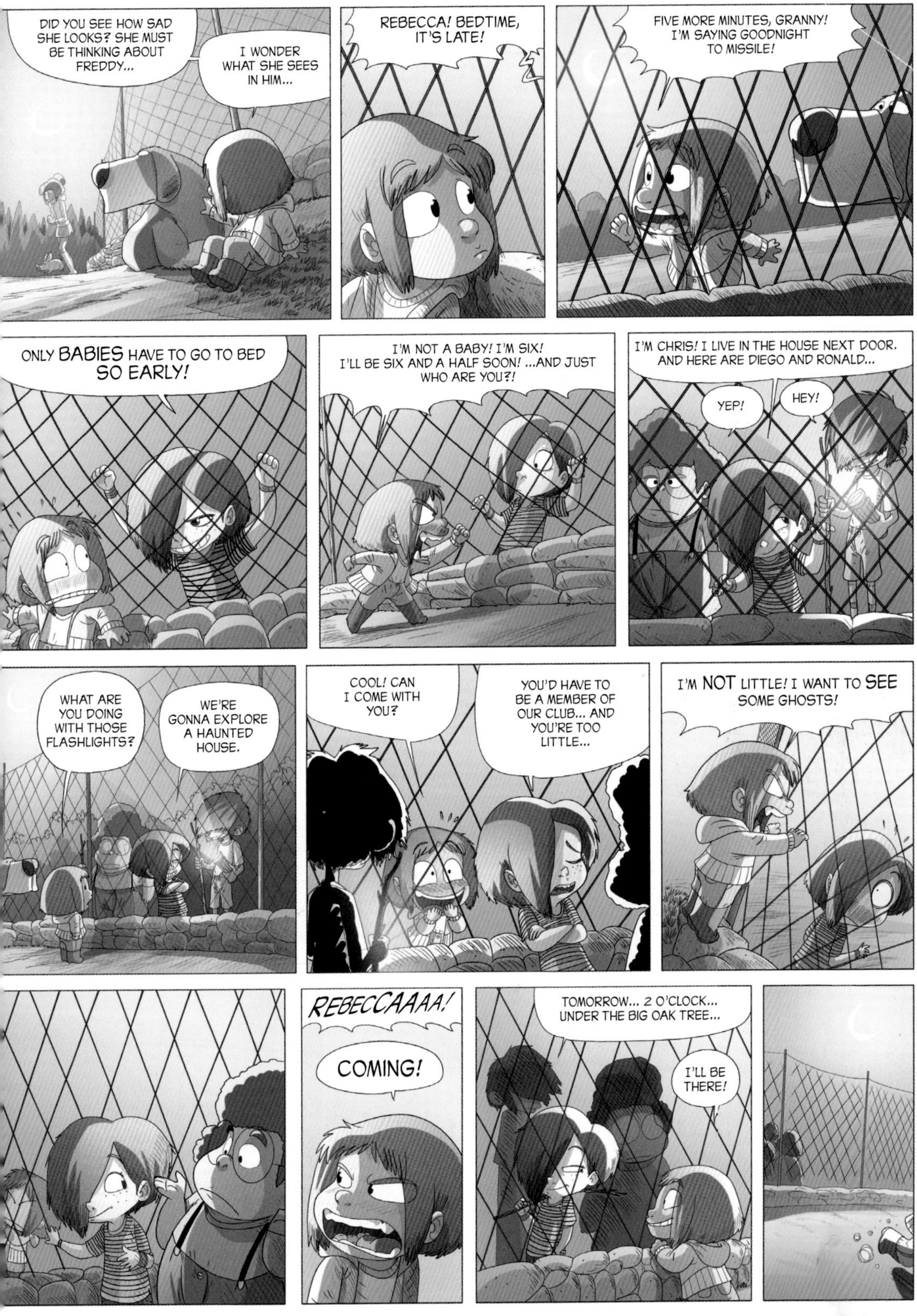
DID YOU SEE HOW SAD SHE LOOKS? SHE MUST BE THINKING ABOUT FREDDY...
I WONDER WHAT SHE SEES IN HIM...
REBECCA! BEDTIME, IT'S LATE!
FIVE MORE MINUTES, GRANNY! I'M SAYING GOODNIGHT TO MISSILE!
ONLY BABIES HAVE TO GO TO BED SO EARLY!
I'M NOT A BABY! I'M SIX! I'LL BE SIX AND A HALF SOON! ...AND JUST WHO ARE YOU?!
I'M CHRIS! I LIVE IN THE HOUSE NEXT DOOR. AND HERE ARE DIEGO AND RONALD...
YEP!
HEY!
WHAT ARE YOU DOING WITH THOSE FLASHLIGHTS?
WE'RE GONNA EXPLORE A HAUNTED HOUSE.
COOL! CAN I COME WITH YOU?
YOU'D HAVE TO BE A MEMBER OF OUR CLUB... AND YOU'RE TOO LITTLE...
I'M NOT LITTLE! I WANT TO SEE SOME GHOSTS!
REBECCAAAA!
COMING!
TOMORROW... 2 O'CLOCK... UNDER THE BIG OAK TREE...
I'LL BE THERE!

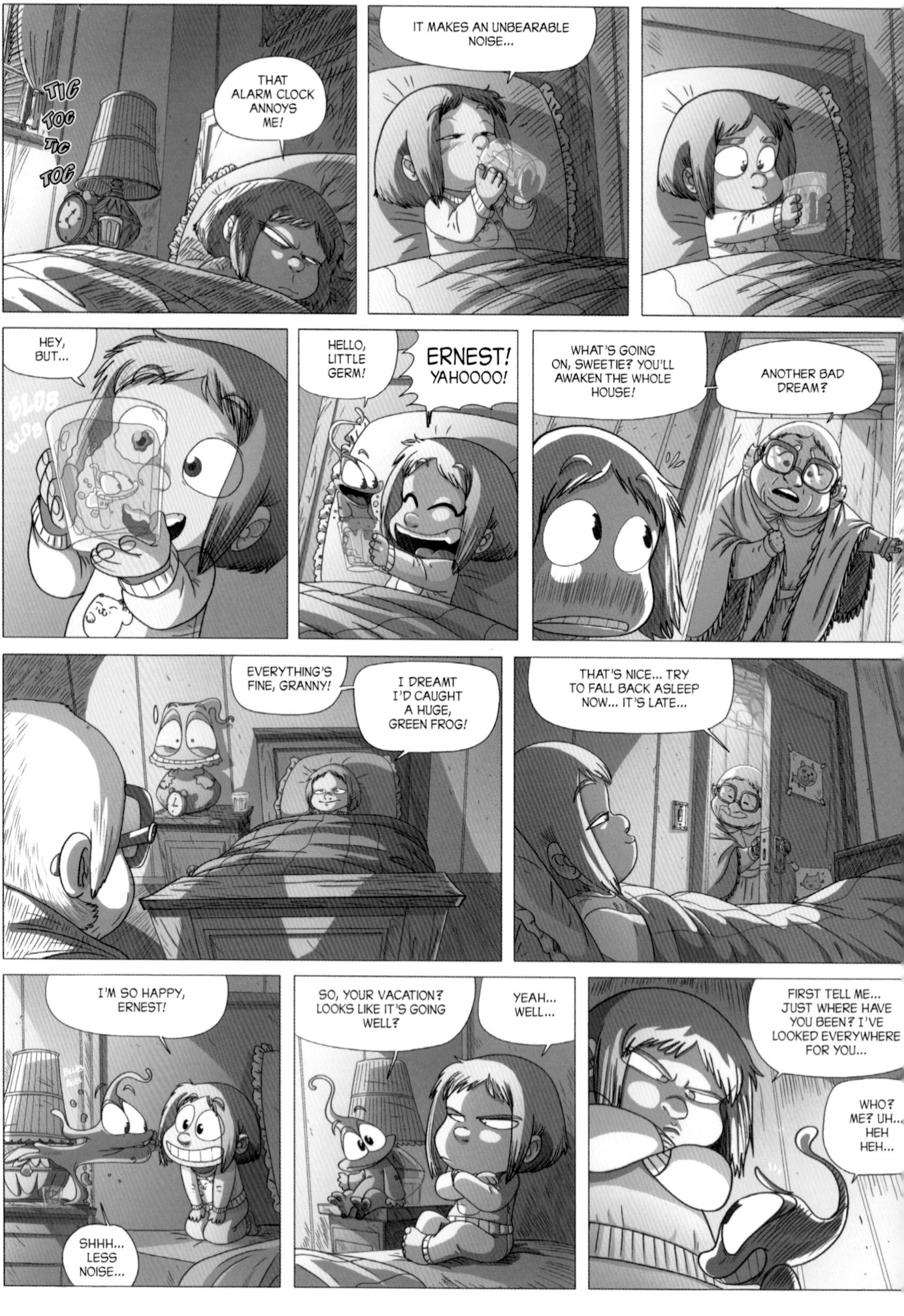
TIC
TOC
TIC
TOC
THAT ALARM CLOCK ANNOYS ME!
IT MAKES AN UNBEARABLE NOISE...
HEY, BUT...
BLOB
BLOB
HELLO, LITTLE GERM!
ERNEST! YAHOOOO!
WHAT'S GOING ON, SWEETIE? YOU'LL AWAKEN THE WHOLE HOUSE!
ANOTHER BAD DREAM?
EVERYTHING'S FINE, GRANNY!
I DREAMT I'D CAUGHT A HUGE, GREEN FROG!
THAT'S NICE... TRY TO FALL BACK ASLEEP NOW... IT'S LATE...
I'M SO HAPPY, ERNEST!
SHHH... LESS NOISE...
SO, YOUR VACATION? LOOKS LIKE IT'S GOING WELL?
YEAH... WELL...
FIRST TELL ME... JUST WHERE HAVE YOU BEEN? I'VE LOOKED EVERYWHERE FOR YOU...
WHO? ME? UH... HEH HEH...

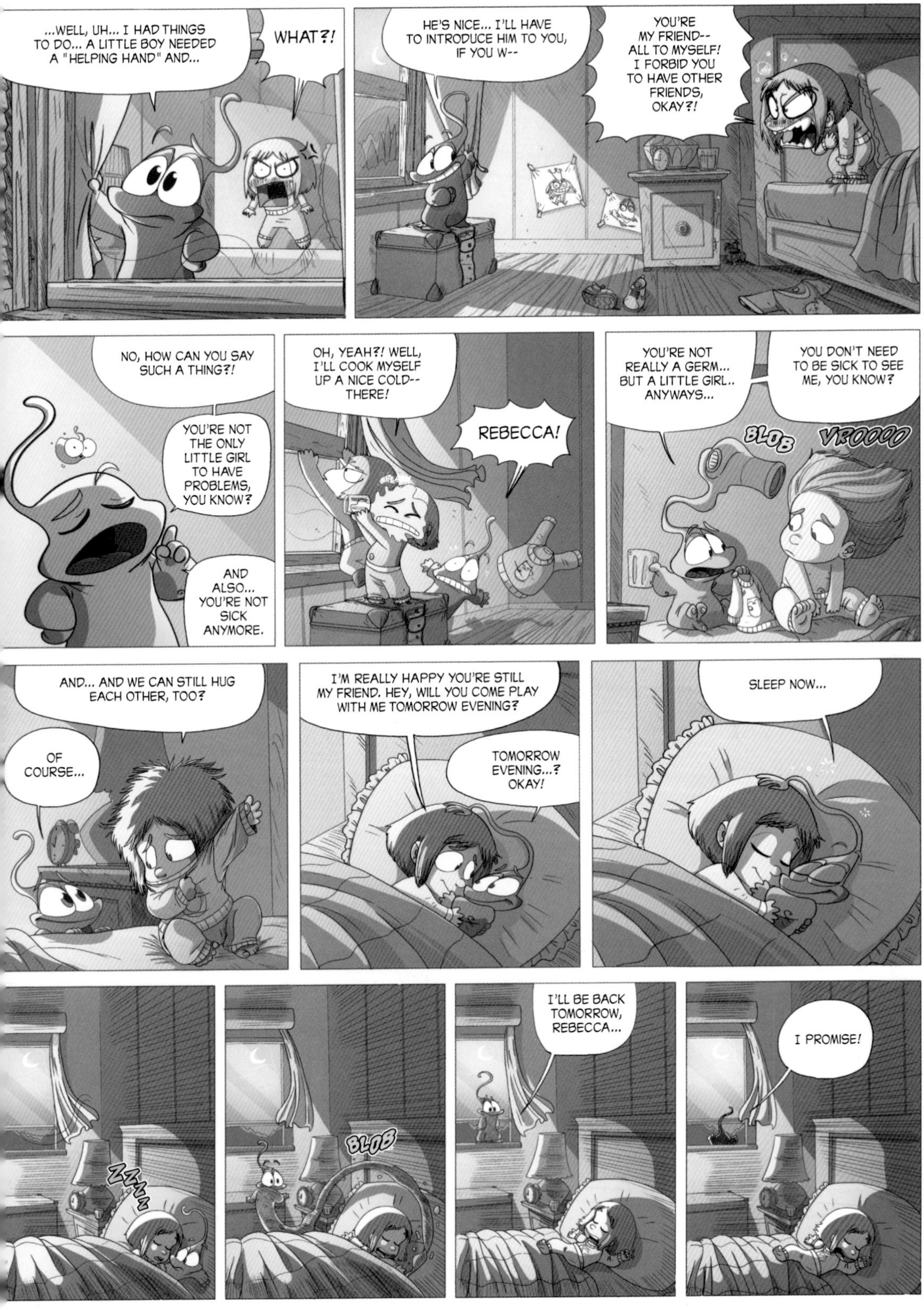
...WELL, UH... I HAD THINGS TO DO... A LITTLE BOY NEEDED A "HELPING HAND" AND...
WHAT?!
HE'S NICE... I'LL HAVE TO INTRODUCE HIM TO YOU, IF YOU W--
YOU'RE MY FRIEND-- ALL TO MYSELF! I FORBID YOU TO HAVE OTHER FRIENDS, OKAY?!
NO, HOW CAN YOU SAY SUCH A THING?!
YOU'RE NOT THE ONLY LITTLE GIRL TO HAVE PROBLEMS, YOU KNOW?
AND ALSO... YOU'RE NOT SICK ANYMORE.
OH, YEAH?! WELL, I'LL COOK MYSELF UP A NICE COLD-- THERE!
REBECCA!
YOU'RE NOT REALLY A GERM... BUT A LITTLE GIRL.. ANYWAYS...
YOU DON'T NEED TO BE SICK TO SEE ME, YOU KNOW?
BLOB
VROOOO
AND... AND WE CAN STILL HUG EACH OTHER, TOO?
OF COURSE...
I'M REALLY HAPPY YOU'RE STILL MY FRIEND. HEY, WILL YOU COME PLAY WITH ME TOMORROW EVENING?
TOMORROW EVENING...? OKAY!
SLEEP NOW...
ZZZZ
BLOB
I'LL BE BACK TOMORROW, REBECCA...
I PROMISE!

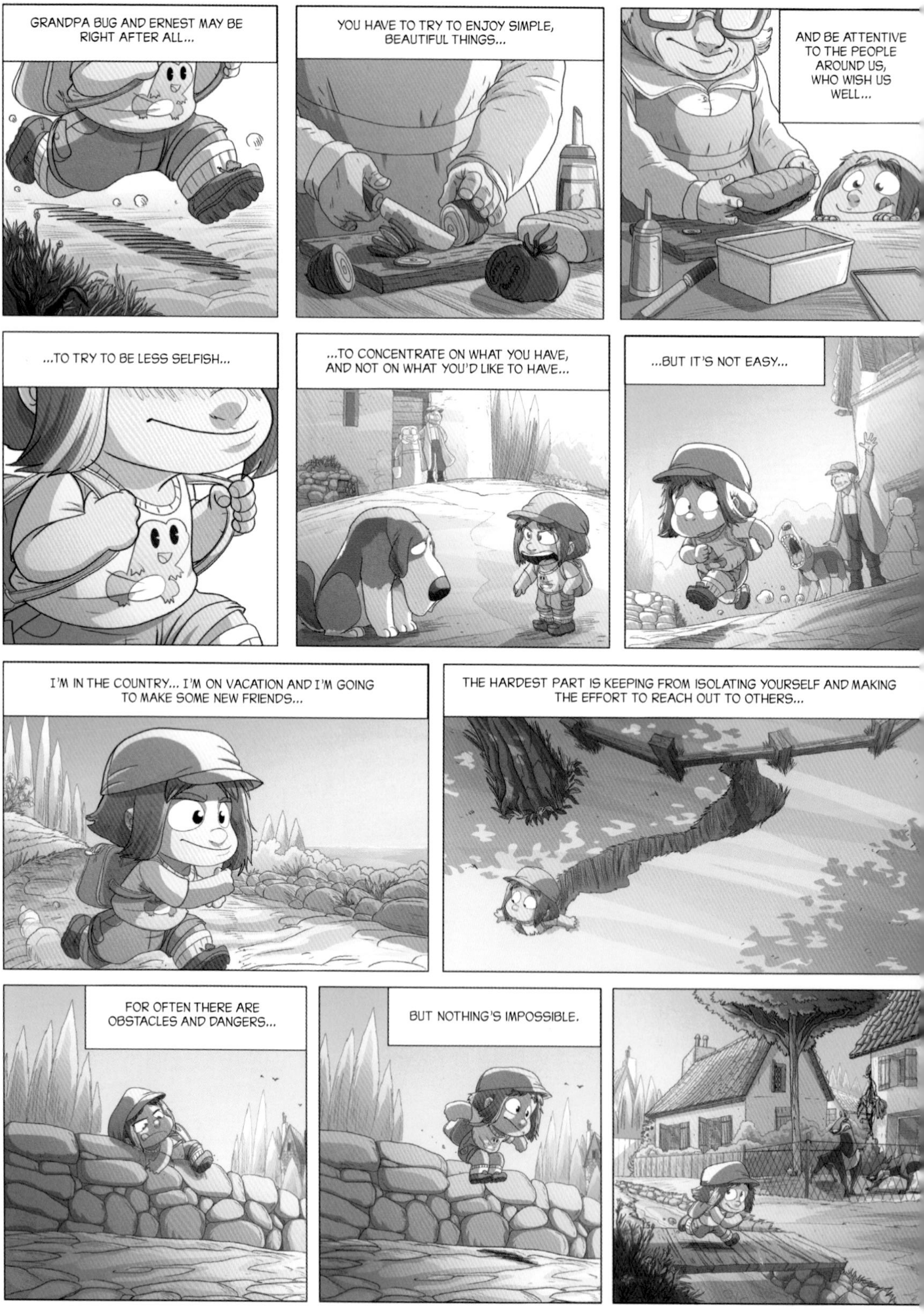

GRANDPA BUG AND ERNEST MAY BE RIGHT AFTER ALL...
YOU HAVE TO TRY TO ENJOY SIMPLE, BEAUTIFUL THINGS...
AND BE ATTENTIVE TO THE PEOPLE AROUND US, WHO WISH US WELL...
...TO TRY TO BE LESS SELFISH...
...TO CONCENTRATE ON WHAT YOU HAVE, AND NOT ON WHAT YOU'D LIKE TO HAVE...
...BUT IT'S NOT EASY...
I'M IN THE COUNTRY... I'M ON VACATION AND I'M GOING TO MAKE SOME NEW FRIENDS...
THE HARDEST PART IS KEEPING FROM ISOLATING YOURSELF AND MAKING THE EFFORT TO REACH OUT TO OTHERS...
FOR OFTEN THERE ARE OBSTACLES AND DANGERS...
BUT NOTHING'S IMPOSSIBLE.

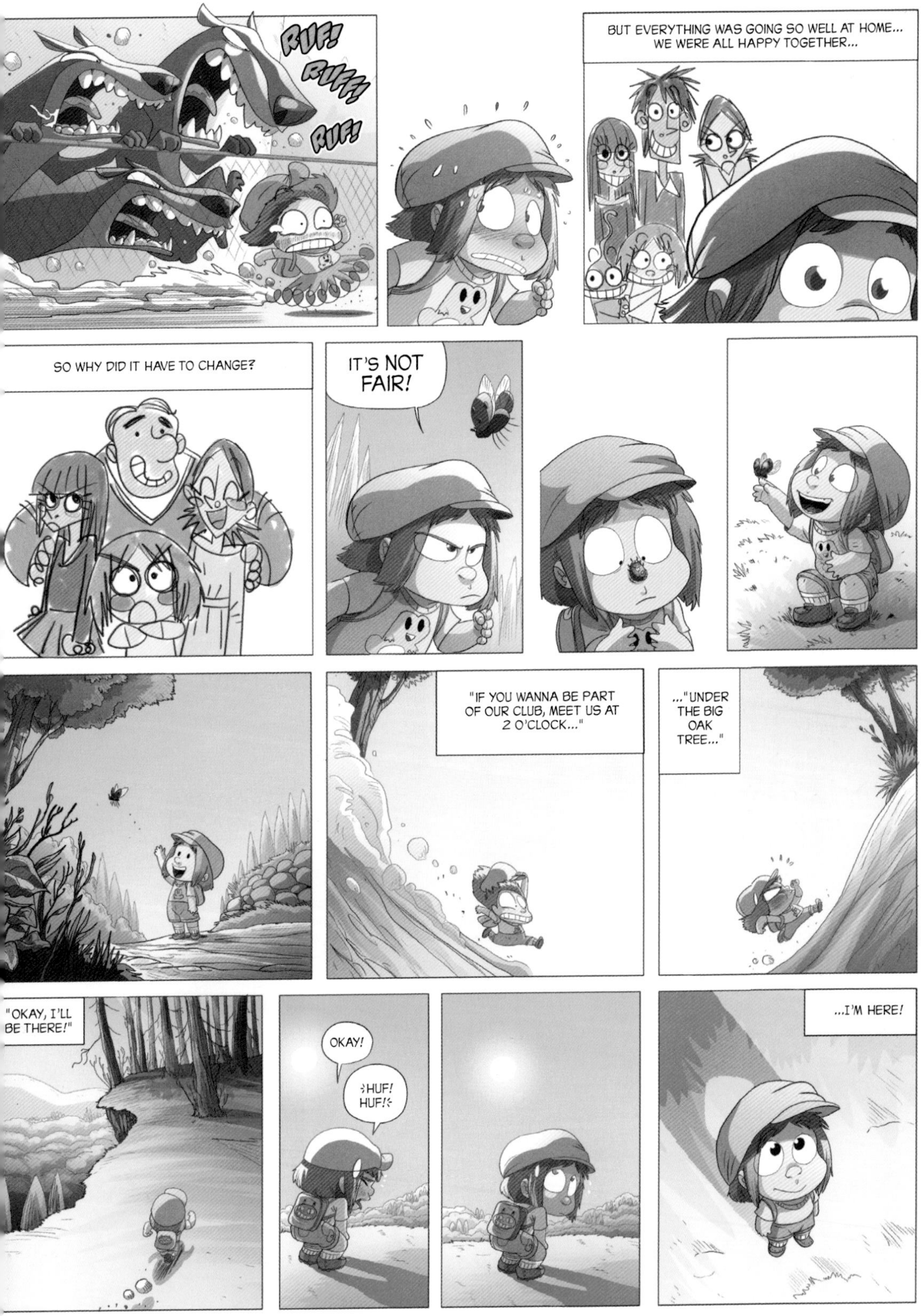
RUF!
RUFF!
RUF!
BUT EVERYTHING WAS GOING SO WELL AT HOME... WE WERE ALL HAPPY TOGETHER...
SO WHY DID IT HAVE TO CHANGE?
IT'S NOT FAIR!
"IF YOU WANNA BE PART OF OUR CLUB, MEET US AT 2 O'CLOCK..."
..."UNDER THE BIG OAK TREE..."
"OKAY, I'LL BE THERE!"
OKAY!
HUF! HUF!
...I'M HERE!

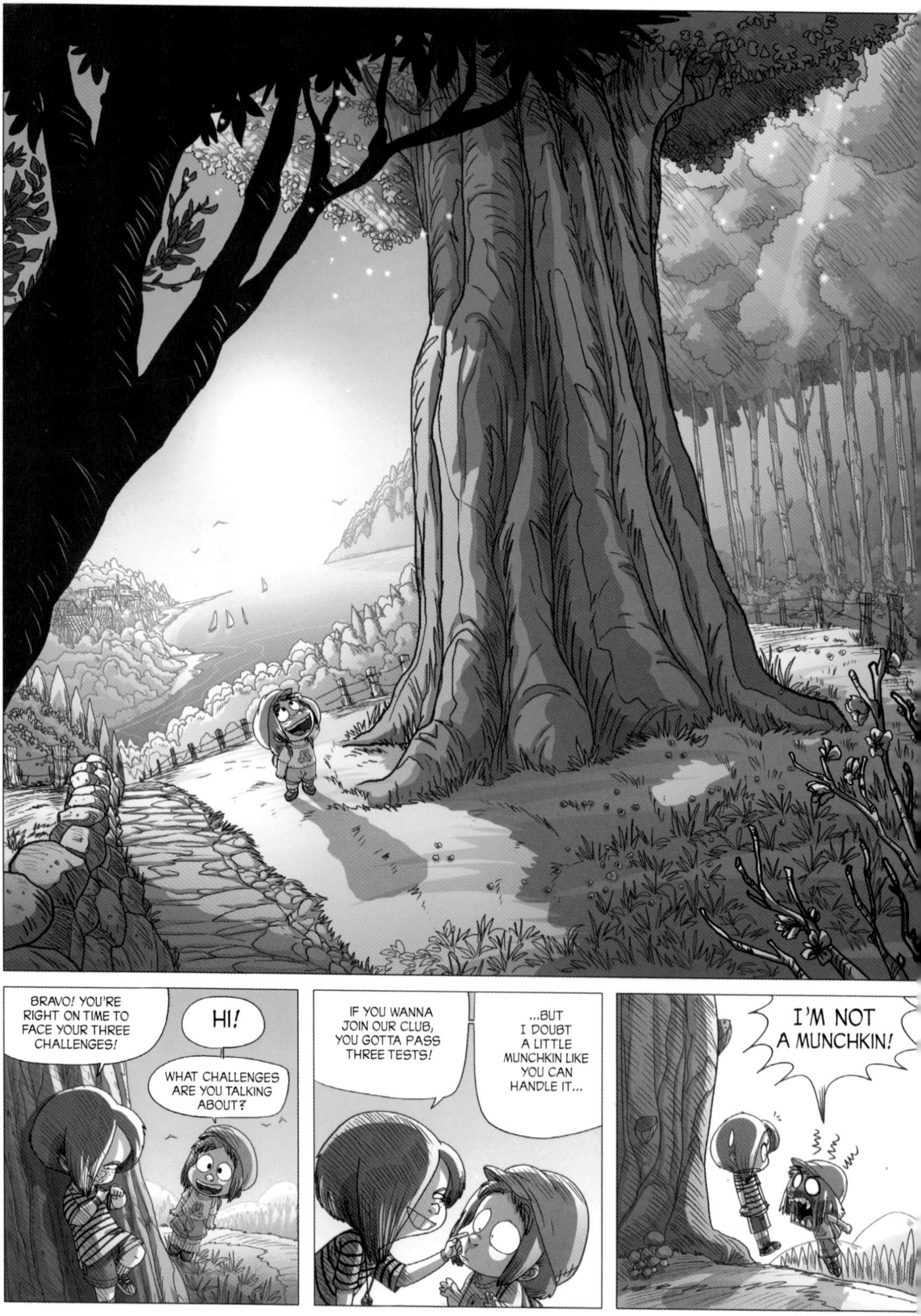
BRAVO! YOU'RE RIGHT ON TIME TO FACE YOUR THREE CHALLENGES!
HI!
WHAT CHALLENGES ARE YOU TALKING ABOUT?
IF YOU WANNA JOIN OUR CLUB, YOU GOTTA PASS THREE TESTS!
...BUT I DOUBT A LITTLE MUNCHKIN LIKE YOU CAN HANDLE IT...
I'M NOT A MUNCHKIN!

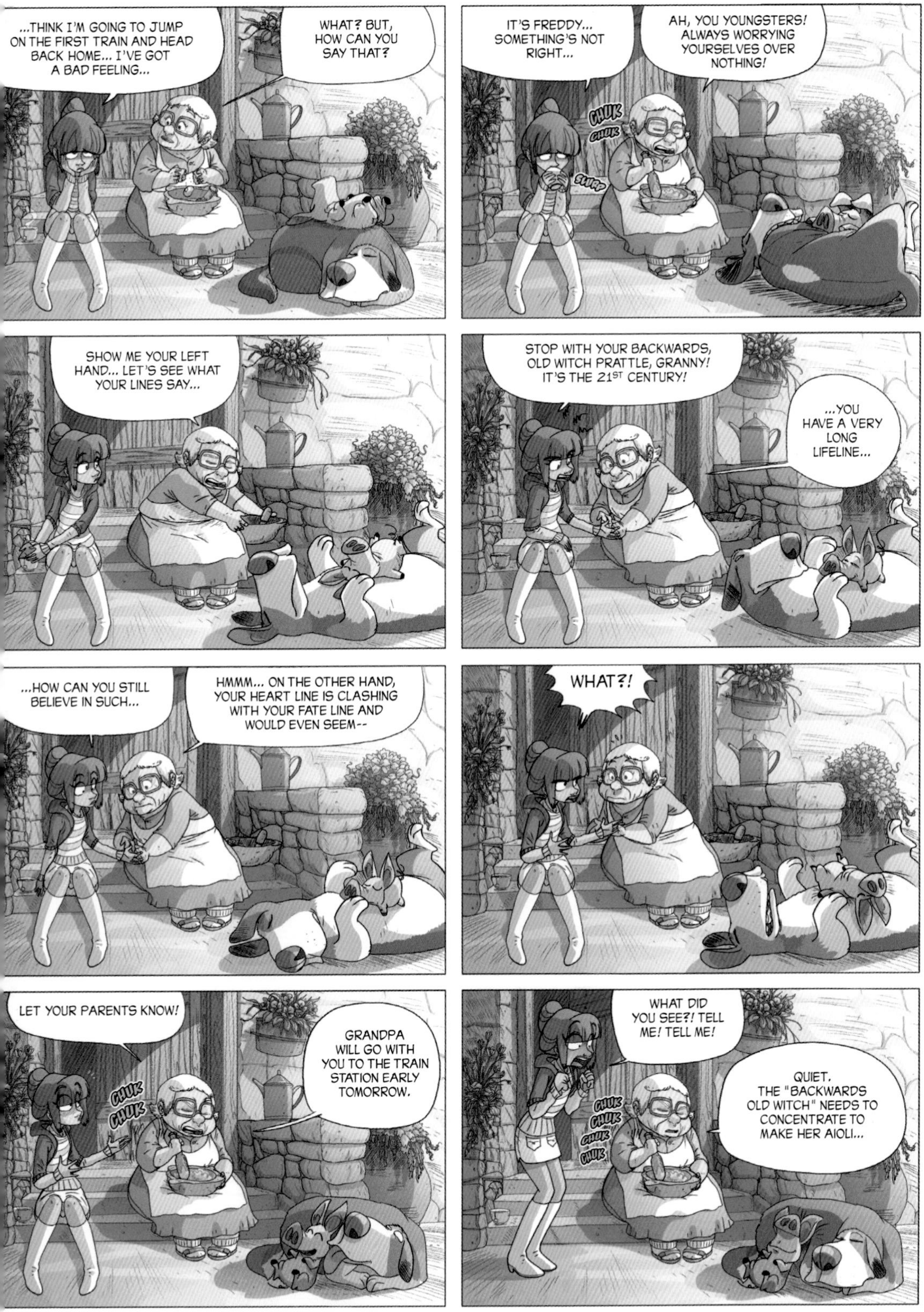
...THINK I'M GOING TO JUMP ON THE FIRST TRAIN AND HEAD BACK HOME... I'VE GOT A BAD FEELING...
WHAT? BUT, HOW CAN YOU SAY THAT?
IT'S FREDDY... SOMETHING'S NOT RIGHT...
AH, YOU YOUNGSTERS! ALWAYS WORRYING YOURSELVES OVER NOTHING!
CHUK
CHUK
SLURP
SHOW ME YOUR LEFT HAND... LET'S SEE WHAT YOUR LINES SAY...
STOP WITH YOUR BACKWARDS, OLD WITCH PRATTLE, GRANNY! IT'S THE 21ST CENTURY!
...YOU HAVE A VERY LONG LIFELINE...
...HOW CAN YOU STILL BELIEVE IN SUCH...
HMMM... ON THE OTHER HAND, YOUR HEART LINE IS CLASHING WITH YOUR FATE LINE AND WOULD EVEN SEEM--
WHAT?!
LET YOUR PARENTS KNOW!
CHUK
CHUK
GRANDPA WILL GO WITH YOU TO THE TRAIN STATION EARLY TOMORROW.
WHAT DID YOU SEE?! TELL ME! TELL ME!
CHUK
CHUK
CHUK
CHUK
QUIET. THE "BACKWARDS OLD WITCH" NEEDS TO CONCENTRATE TO MAKE HER AIOLI...

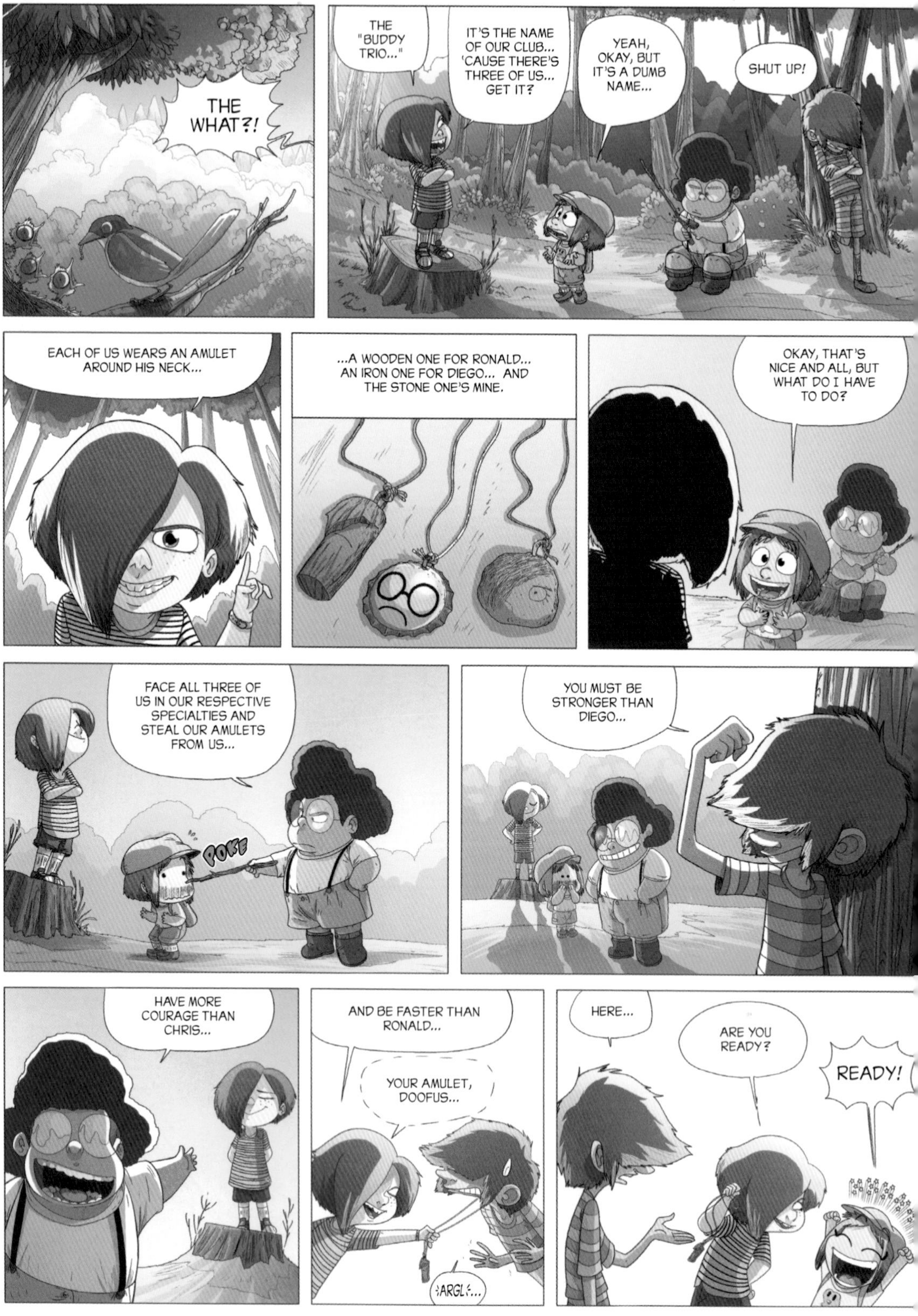
THE WHAT?!
THE "BUDDY TRIO..."
IT'S THE NAME OF OUR CLUB... 'CAUSE THERE'S THREE OF US... GET IT?
YEAH, OKAY, BUT IT'S A DUMB NAME...
SHUT UP!
EACH OF US WEARS AN AMULET AROUND HIS NECK...
...A WOODEN ONE FOR RONALD... AN IRON ONE FOR DIEGO... AND THE STONE ONE'S MINE.
OKAY, THAT'S NICE AND ALL, BUT WHAT DO I HAVE TO DO?
FACE ALL THREE OF US IN OUR RESPECTIVE SPECIALTIES AND STEAL OUR AMULETS FROM US...
POKE
YOU MUST BE STRONGER THAN DIEGO...
HAVE MORE COURAGE THAN CHRIS...
AND BE FASTER THAN RONALD...
YOUR AMULET, DOOFUS...
ARGL...
HERE...
ARE YOU READY?
READY!

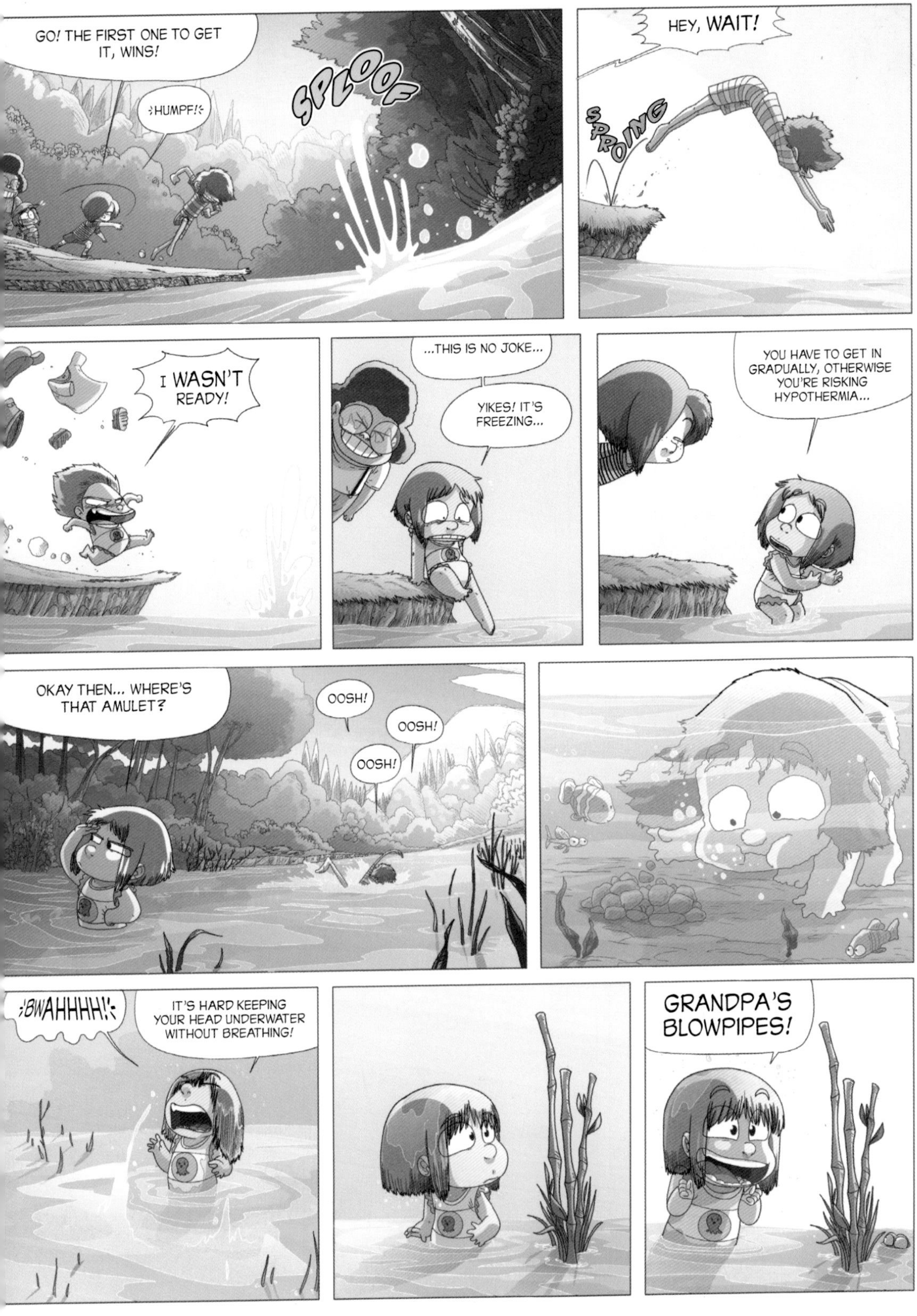
GO! THE FIRST ONE TO GET IT, WINS!
HUMPF!
SPLOOF
HEY, WAIT!
SPROING
I WASN'T READY!
...THIS IS NO JOKE...
YIKES! IT'S FREEZING...
YOU HAVE TO GET IN GRADUALLY, OTHERWISE YOU'RE RISKING HYPOTHERMIA...
OKAY THEN... WHERE'S THAT AMULET?
OOSH!
OOSH!
OOSH!
BWAHHHH!
IT'S HARD KEEPING YOUR HEAD UNDERWATER WITHOUT BREATHING!
GRANDPA'S BLOWPIPES!

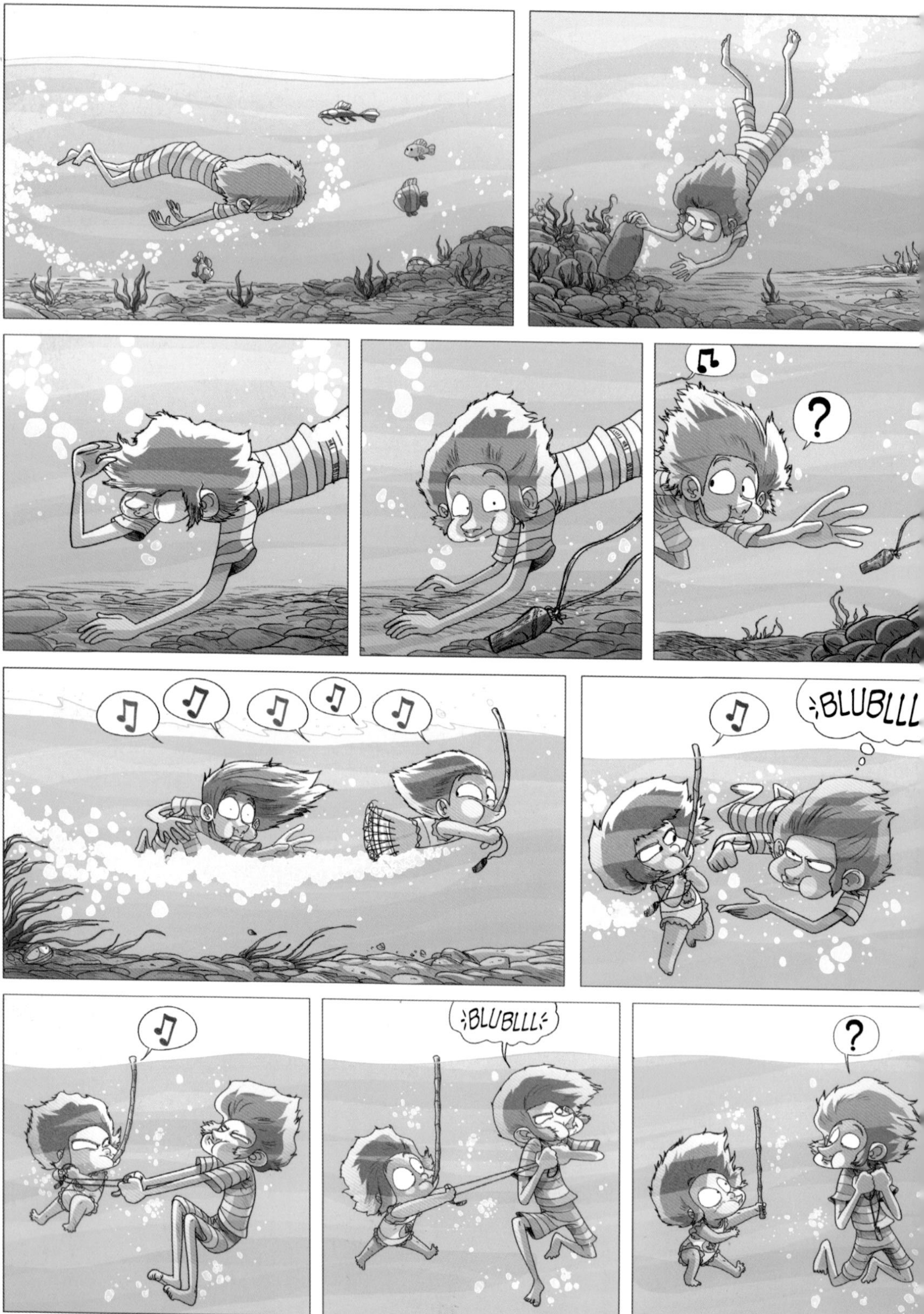
♫
?
♫
♫
♫
♫
♫
♫
BLUBLLL
♫
BLUBLLL
?

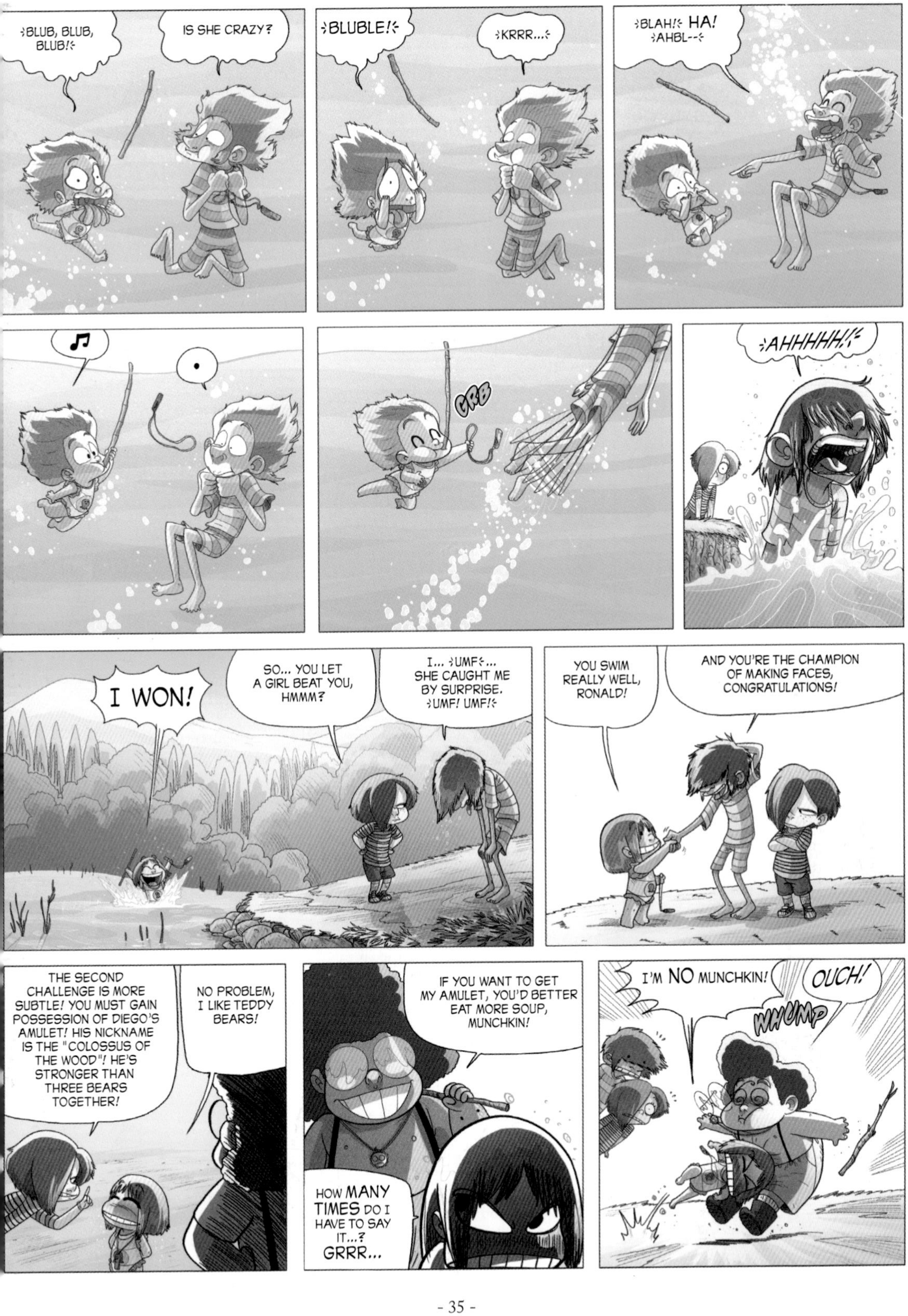
BLUB, BLUB, BLUB!
IS SHE CRAZY?
BLUBLE!
KRRR...
BLAH! HA! AHBL--
GRB
AHHHHH!
I WON!
SO... YOU LET A GIRL BEAT YOU, HMMM?
I... UMF... SHE CAUGHT ME BY SURPRISE. UMF! UMF!
YOU SWIM REALLY WELL, RONALD!
AND YOU'RE THE CHAMPION OF MAKING FACES, CONGRATULATIONS!
THE SECOND CHALLENGE IS MORE SUBTLE! YOU MUST GAIN POSSESSION OF DIEGO'S AMULET! HIS NICKNAME IS THE "COLOSSUS OF THE WOOD"! HE'S STRONGER THAN THREE BEARS TOGETHER!
NO PROBLEM, I LIKE TEDDY BEARS!
IF YOU WANT TO GET MY AMULET, YOU'D BETTER EAT MORE SOUP, MUNCHKIN!
HOW MANY TIMES DO I HAVE TO SAY IT...? GRRR...
I'M NO MUNCHKIN!
OUCH!
WHUMP

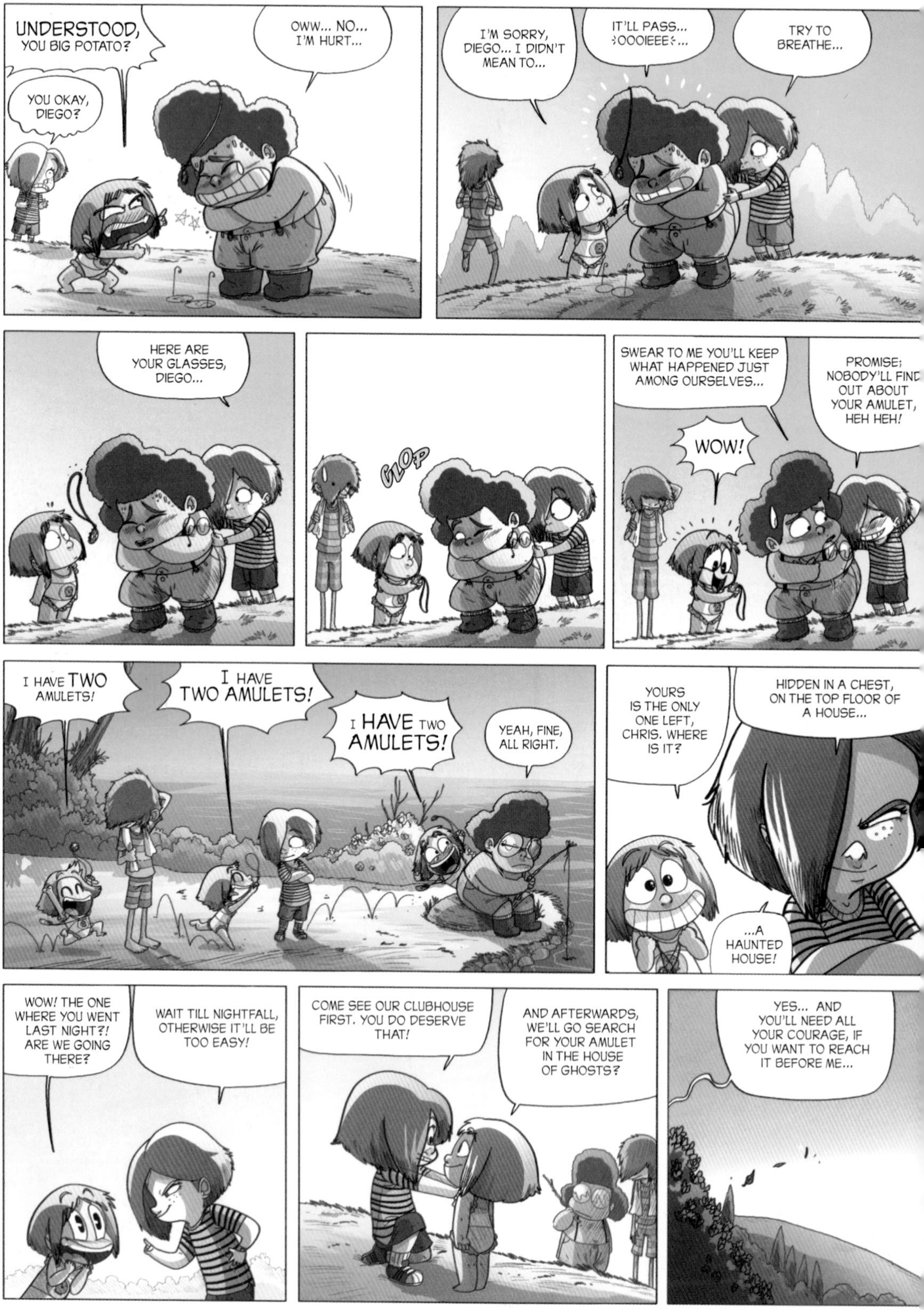

UNDERSTOOD, YOU BIG POTATO?
YOU OKAY, DIEGO?
OWW... NO... I'M HURT...
I'M SORRY, DIEGO... I DIDN'T MEAN TO...
IT'LL PASS... OOOIEEE...
TRY TO BREATHE...
HERE ARE YOUR GLASSES, DIEGO...
GLOP
SWEAR TO ME YOU'LL KEEP WHAT HAPPENED JUST AMONG OURSELVES...
WOW!
PROMISE; NOBODY'LL FIND OUT ABOUT YOUR AMULET, HEH HEH!
I HAVE TWO AMULETS!
I HAVE TWO AMULETS!
I HAVE TWO AMULETS!
YEAH, FINE, ALL RIGHT.
YOURS IS THE ONLY ONE LEFT, CHRIS. WHERE IS IT?
HIDDEN IN A CHEST, ON THE TOP FLOOR OF A HOUSE...
...A HAUNTED HOUSE!
WOW! THE ONE WHERE YOU WENT LAST NIGHT?! ARE WE GOING THERE?
WAIT TILL NIGHTFALL, OTHERWISE IT'LL BE TOO EASY!
COME SEE OUR CLUBHOUSE FIRST. YOU DO DESERVE THAT!
AND AFTERWARDS, WE'LL GO SEARCH FOR YOUR AMULET IN THE HOUSE OF GHOSTS?
YES... AND YOU'LL NEED ALL YOUR COURAGE, IF YOU WANT TO REACH IT BEFORE ME...

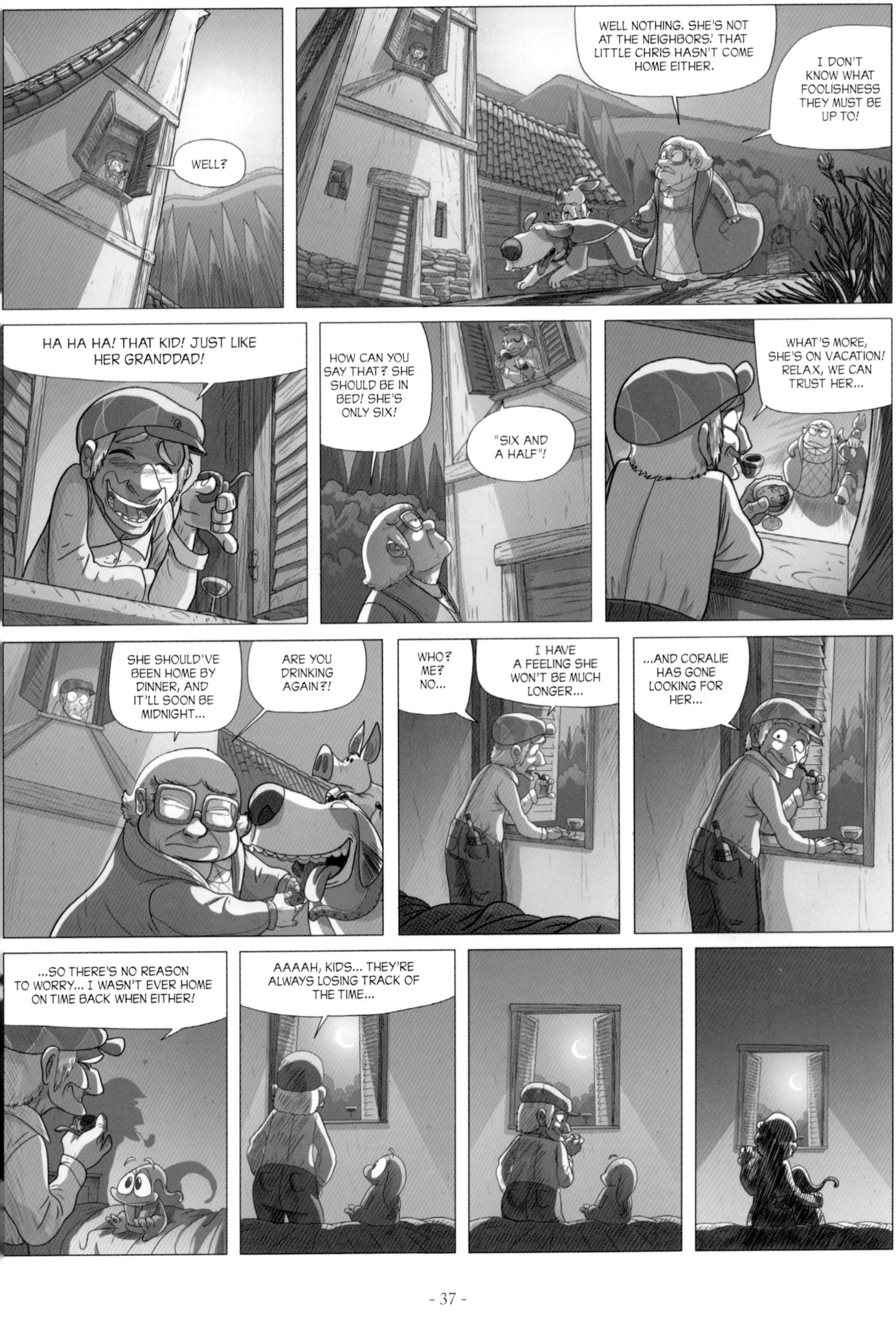
WELL?
WELL NOTHING. SHE'S NOT AT THE NEIGHBORS! THAT LITTLE CHRIS HASN'T COME HOME EITHER.
I DON'T KNOW WHAT FOOLISHNESS THEY MUST BE UP TO!
HA HA HA! THAT KID! JUST LIKE HER GRANDDAD!
HOW CAN YOU SAY THAT? SHE SHOULD BE IN BED! SHE'S ONLY SIX!
"SIX AND A HALF"!
WHAT'S MORE, SHE'S ON VACATION! RELAX, WE CAN TRUST HER...
SHE SHOULD'VE BEEN HOME BY DINNER, AND IT'LL SOON BE MIDNIGHT...
ARE YOU DRINKING AGAIN?!
WHO? ME? NO...
I HAVE A FEELING SHE WON'T BE MUCH LONGER...
...AND CORALIE HAS GONE LOOKING FOR HER...
...SO THERE'S NO REASON TO WORRY... I WASN'T EVER HOME ON TIME BACK WHEN EITHER!
AAAAH, KIDS... THEY'RE ALWAYS LOSING TRACK OF THE TIME...

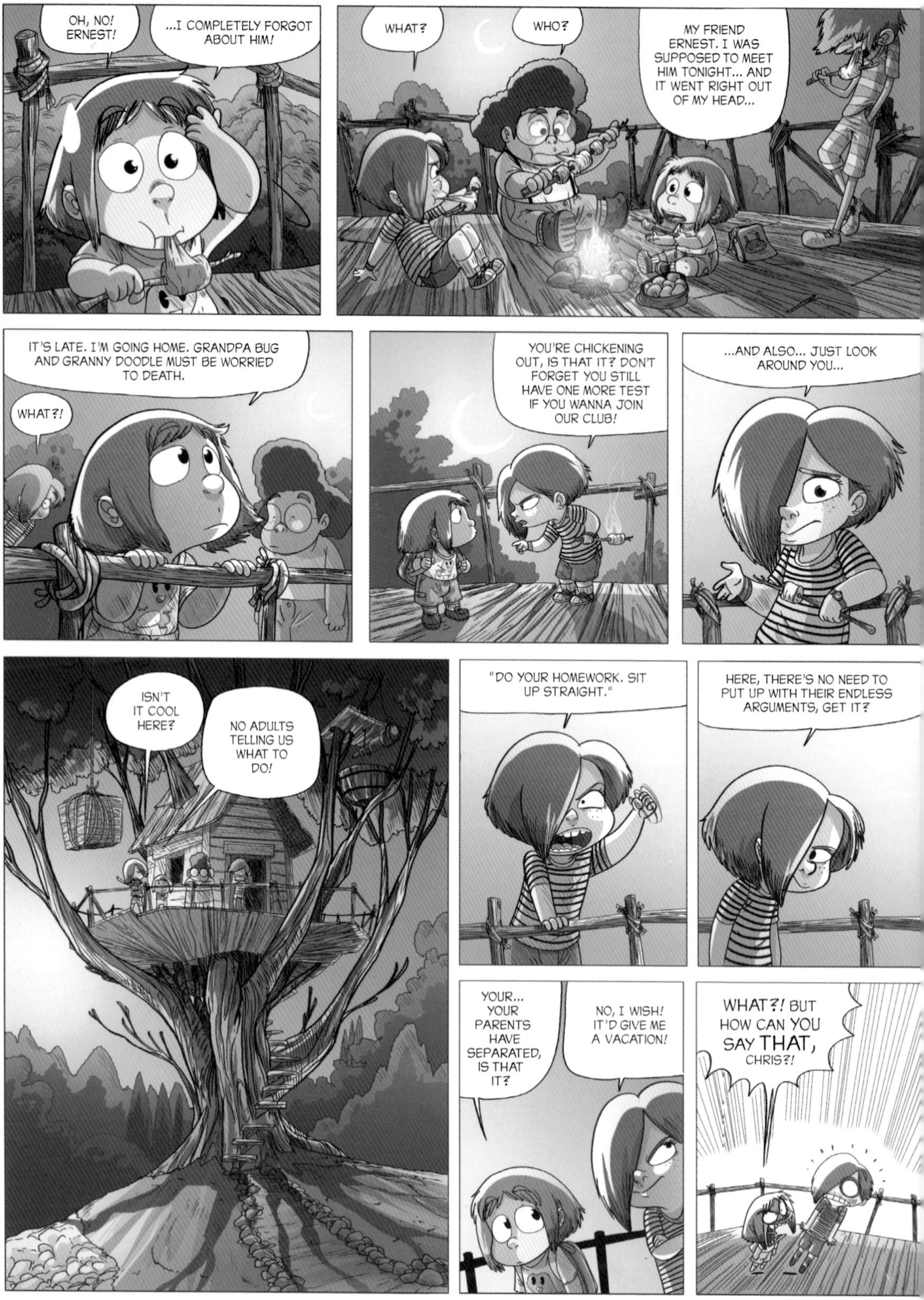
OH, NO! ERNEST!
...I COMPLETELY FORGOT ABOUT HIM!
WHAT?
WHO?
MY FRIEND ERNEST. I WAS SUPPOSED TO MEET HIM TONIGHT... AND IT WENT RIGHT OUT OF MY HEAD...
IT'S LATE. I'M GOING HOME. GRANDPA BUG AND GRANNY DOODLE MUST BE WORRIED TO DEATH.
WHAT?!
YOU'RE CHICKENING OUT, IS THAT IT? DON'T FORGET YOU STILL HAVE ONE MORE TEST IF YOU WANNA JOIN OUR CLUB!
...AND ALSO... JUST LOOK AROUND YOU...
ISN'T IT COOL HERE?
NO ADULTS TELLING US WHAT TO DO!
"DO YOUR HOMEWORK. SIT UP STRAIGHT."
HERE, THERE'S NO NEED TO PUT UP WITH THEIR ENDLESS ARGUMENTS, GET IT?
YOUR... YOUR PARENTS HAVE SEPARATED, IS THAT IT?
NO, I WISH! IT'D GIVE ME A VACATION!
WHAT?! BUT HOW CAN YOU SAY THAT, CHRIS?!

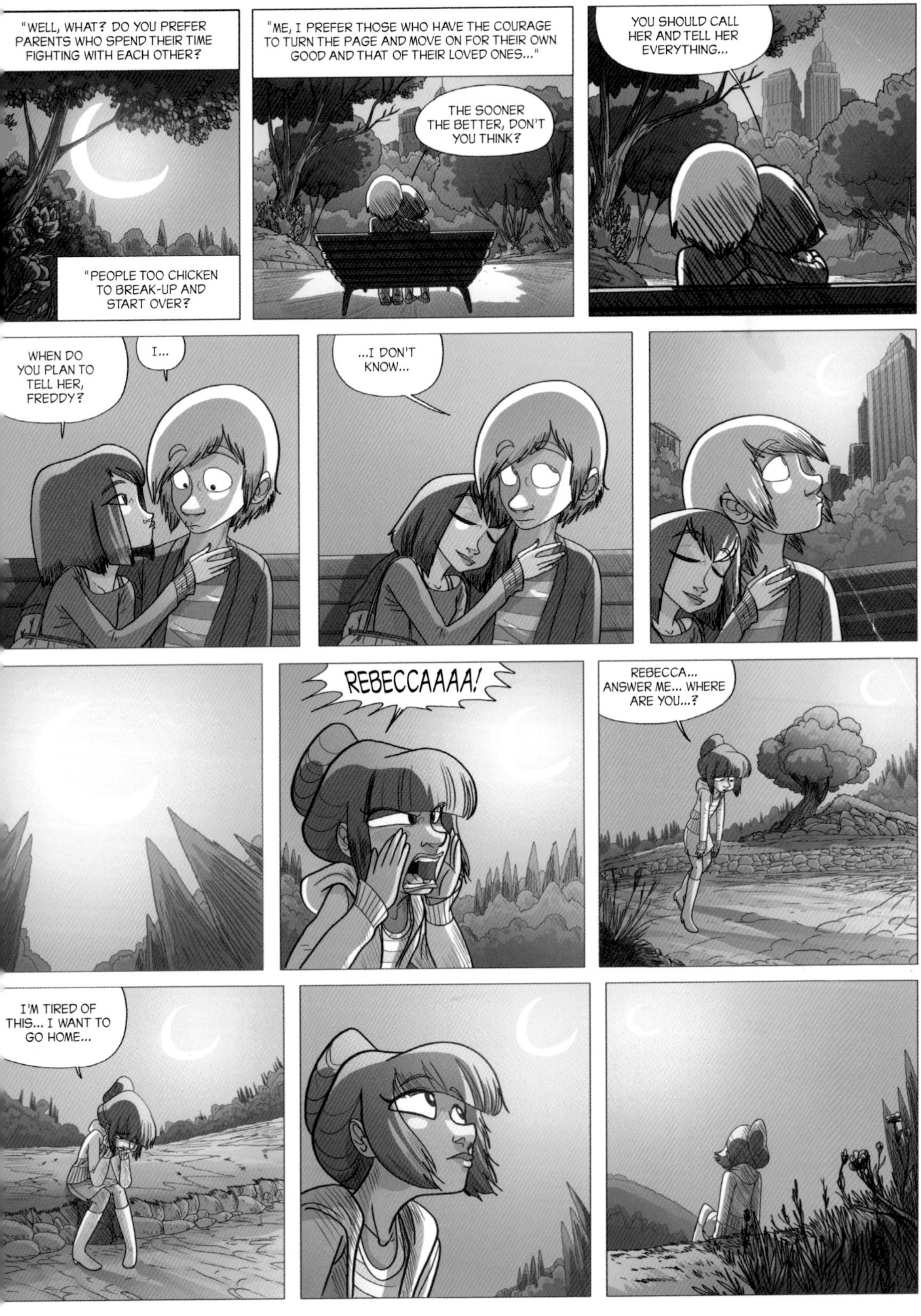

"WELL, WHAT? DO YOU PREFER PARENTS WHO SPEND THEIR TIME FIGHTING WITH EACH OTHER?
"PEOPLE TOO CHICKEN TO BREAK-UP AND START OVER?
"ME, I PREFER THOSE WHO HAVE THE COURAGE TO TURN THE PAGE AND MOVE ON FOR THEIR OWN GOOD AND THAT OF THEIR LOVED ONES..."
THE SOONER THE BETTER, DON'T YOU THINK?
YOU SHOULD CALL HER AND TELL HER EVERYTHING...
WHEN DO YOU PLAN TO TELL HER, FREDDY?
I...
...I DON'T KNOW...
REBECCAAAA!
REBECCA... ANSWER ME... WHERE ARE YOU...?
I'M TIRED OF THIS... I WANT TO GO HOME...

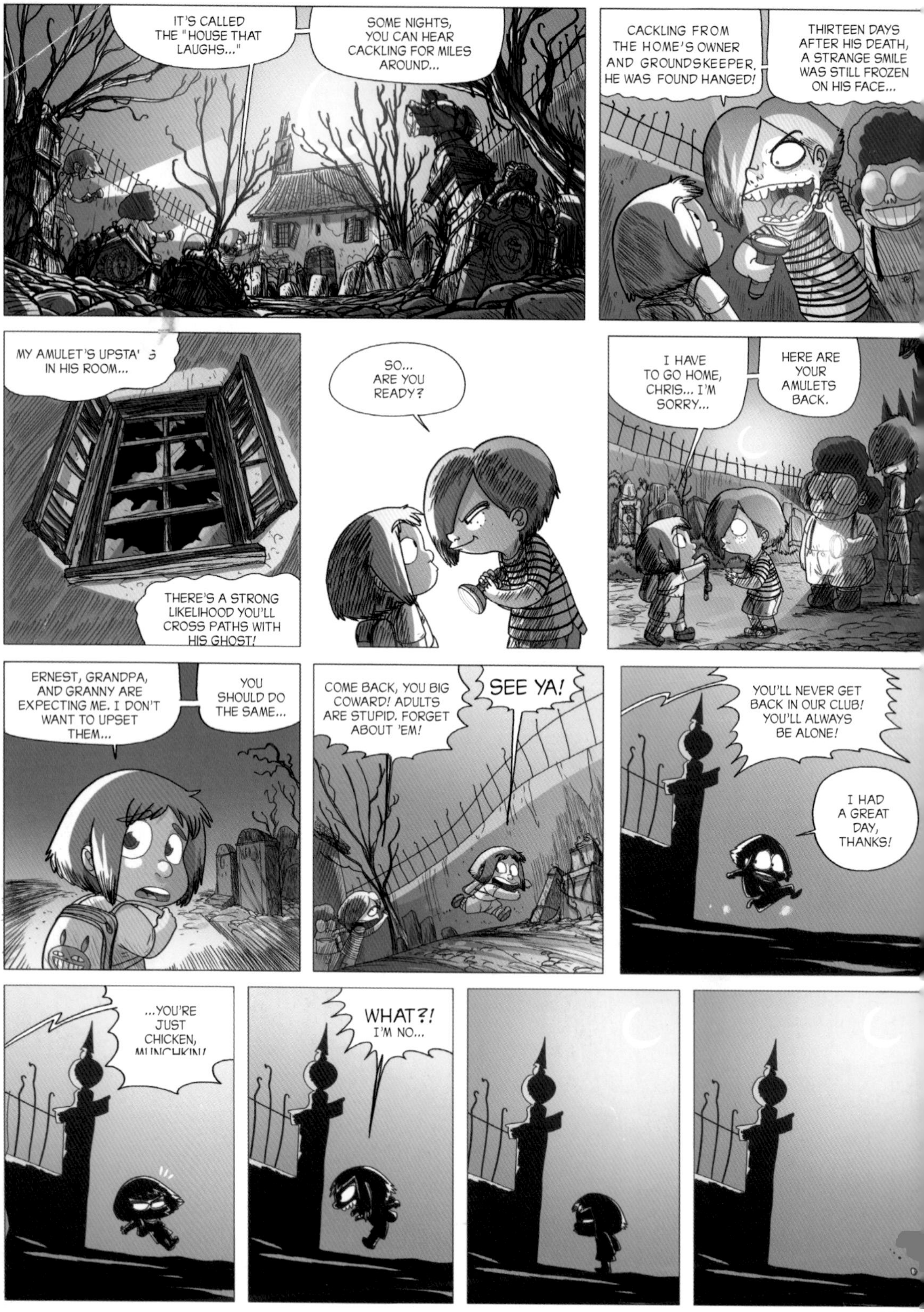
IT'S CALLED THE "HOUSE THAT LAUGHS..."
SOME NIGHTS, YOU CAN HEAR CACKLING FOR MILES AROUND...
CACKLING FROM THE HOME'S OWNER AND GROUNDSKEEPER. HE WAS FOUND HANGED!
THIRTEEN DAYS AFTER HIS DEATH, A STRANGE SMILE WAS STILL FROZEN ON HIS FACE...
MY AMULET'S UPSTA' 'S IN HIS ROOM...
THERE'S A STRONG LIKELIHOOD YOU'LL CROSS PATHS WITH HIS GHOST!
SO... ARE YOU READY?
I HAVE TO GO HOME, CHRIS... I'M SORRY...
HERE ARE YOUR AMULETS BACK.
ERNEST, GRANDPA, AND GRANNY ARE EXPECTING ME. I DON'T WANT TO UPSET THEM...
YOU SHOULD DO THE SAME...
COME BACK, YOU BIG COWARD! ADULTS ARE STUPID. FORGET ABOUT 'EM!
SEE YA!
YOU'LL NEVER GET BACK IN OUR CLUB! YOU'LL ALWAYS BE ALONE!
I HAD A GREAT DAY, THANKS!
...YOU'RE JUST CHICKEN, MUNCHKIN!
WHAT?! I'M NO...

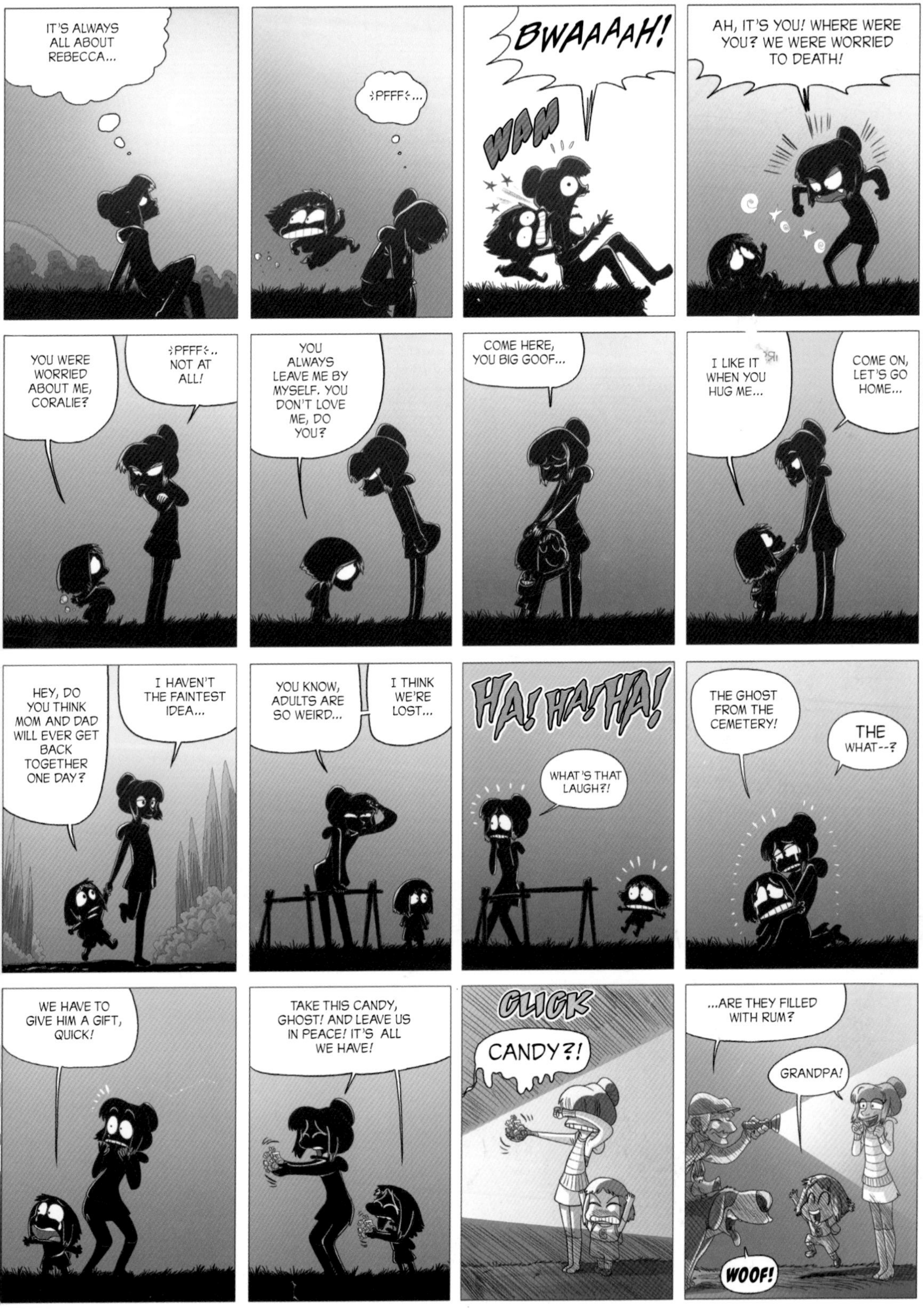
IT'S ALWAYS ALL ABOUT REBECCA...
⁏PFFF⁏...
BWAAAAH!
WAM
AH, IT'S YOU! WHERE WERE YOU? WE WERE WORRIED TO DEATH!
YOU WERE WORRIED ABOUT ME, CORALIE?
⁏PFFF⁏.. NOT AT ALL!
YOU ALWAYS LEAVE ME BY MYSELF. YOU DON'T LOVE ME, DO YOU?
COME HERE, YOU BIG GOOF...
I LIKE IT WHEN YOU HUG ME...
COME ON, LET'S GO HOME...
HEY, DO YOU THINK MOM AND DAD WILL EVER GET BACK TOGETHER ONE DAY?
I HAVEN'T THE FAINTEST IDEA...
YOU KNOW, ADULTS ARE SO WEIRD...
I THINK WE'RE LOST...
HA! HA! HA!
WHAT'S THAT LAUGH?!
THE GHOST FROM THE CEMETERY!
THE WHAT--?
WE HAVE TO GIVE HIM A GIFT, QUICK!
TAKE THIS CANDY, GHOST! AND LEAVE US IN PEACE! IT'S ALL WE HAVE!
CLICK
CANDY?!
...ARE THEY FILLED WITH RUM?
GRANDPA!
WOOF!

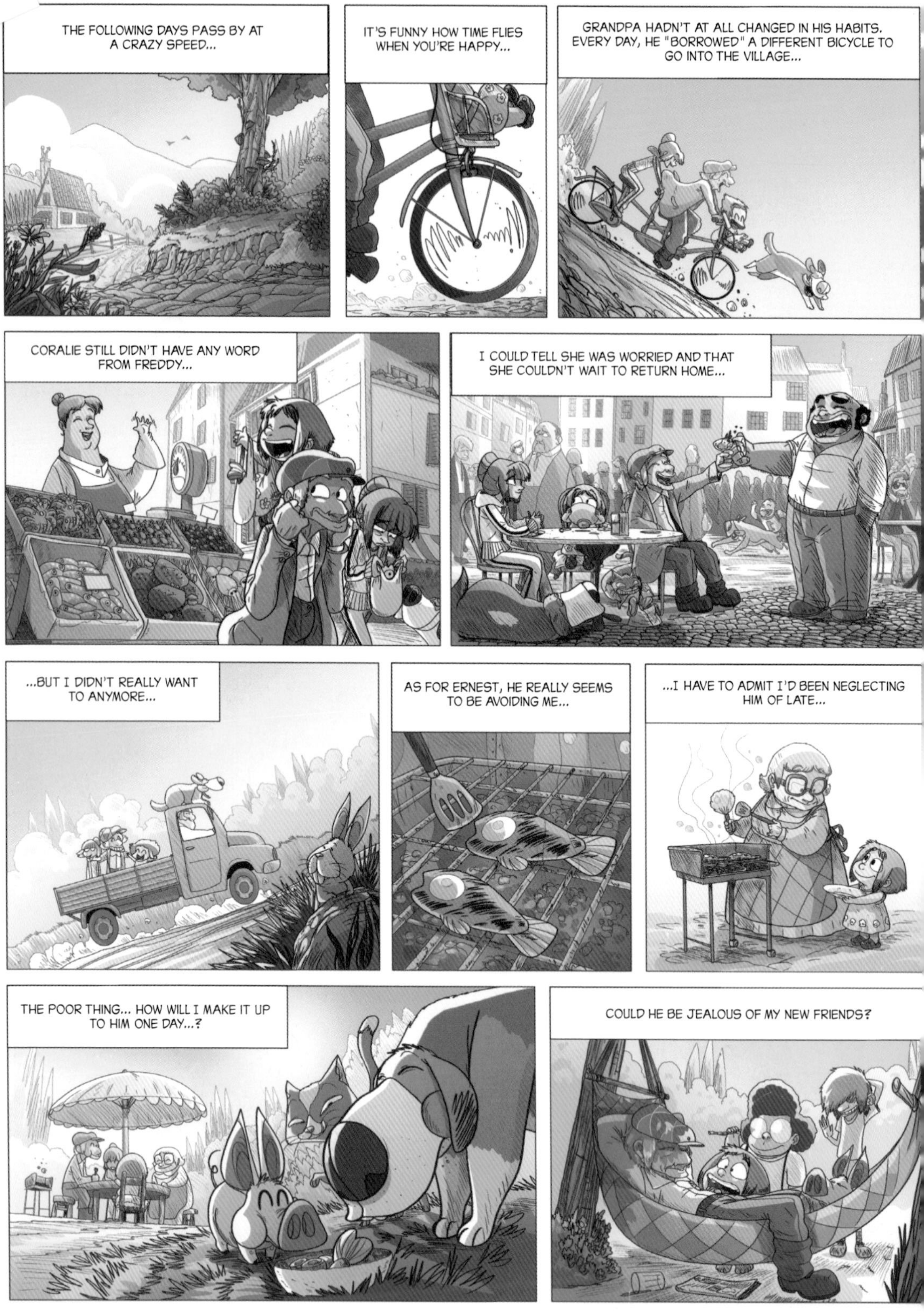
THE FOLLOWING DAYS PASS BY AT A CRAZY SPEED...
IT'S FUNNY HOW TIME FLIES WHEN YOU'RE HAPPY...
GRANDPA HADN'T AT ALL CHANGED IN HIS HABITS. EVERY DAY, HE "BORROWED" A DIFFERENT BICYCLE TO GO INTO THE VILLAGE...
CORALIE STILL DIDN'T HAVE ANY WORD FROM FREDDY...
I COULD TELL SHE WAS WORRIED AND THAT SHE COULDN'T WAIT TO RETURN HOME...
...BUT I DIDN'T REALLY WANT TO ANYMORE...
AS FOR ERNEST, HE REALLY SEEMS TO BE AVOIDING ME...
...I HAVE TO ADMIT I'D BEEN NEGLECTING HIM OF LATE...
THE POOR THING... HOW WILL I MAKE IT UP TO HIM ONE DAY...?
COULD HE BE JEALOUS OF MY NEW FRIENDS?

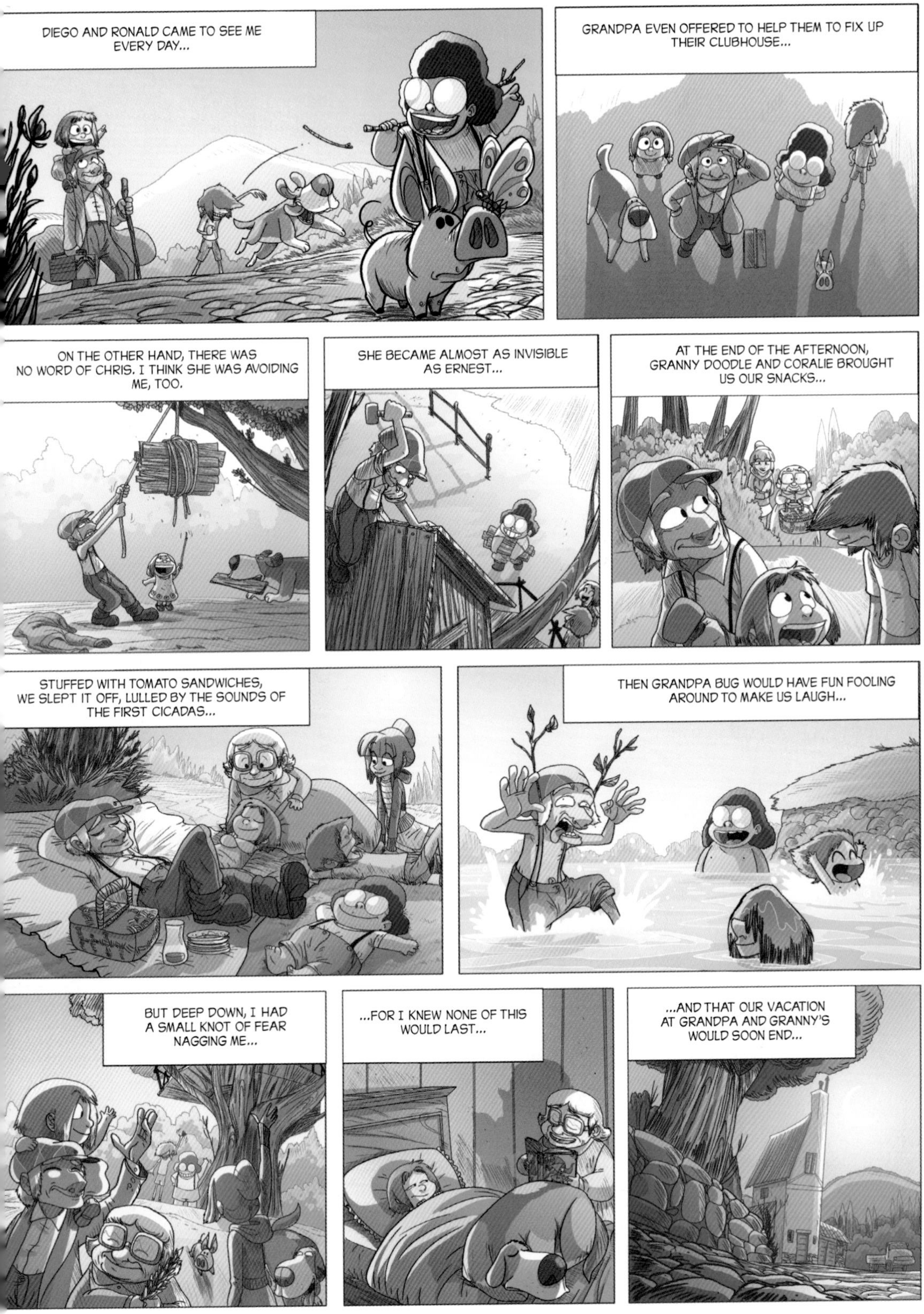
DIEGO AND RONALD CAME TO SEE ME EVERY DAY...
GRANDPA EVEN OFFERED TO HELP THEM TO FIX UP THEIR CLUBHOUSE...
ON THE OTHER HAND, THERE WAS NO WORD OF CHRIS. I THINK SHE WAS AVOIDING ME, TOO.
SHE BECAME ALMOST AS INVISIBLE AS ERNEST...
AT THE END OF THE AFTERNOON, GRANNY DOODLE AND CORALIE BROUGHT US OUR SNACKS...
STUFFED WITH TOMATO SANDWICHES, WE SLEPT IT OFF, LULLED BY THE SOUNDS OF THE FIRST CICADAS...
THEN GRANDPA BUG WOULD HAVE FUN FOOLING AROUND TO MAKE US LAUGH...
BUT DEEP DOWN, I HAD A SMALL KNOT OF FEAR NAGGING ME...
...FOR I KNEW NONE OF THIS WOULD LAST...
...AND THAT OUR VACATION AT GRANDPA AND GRANNY'S WOULD SOON END...

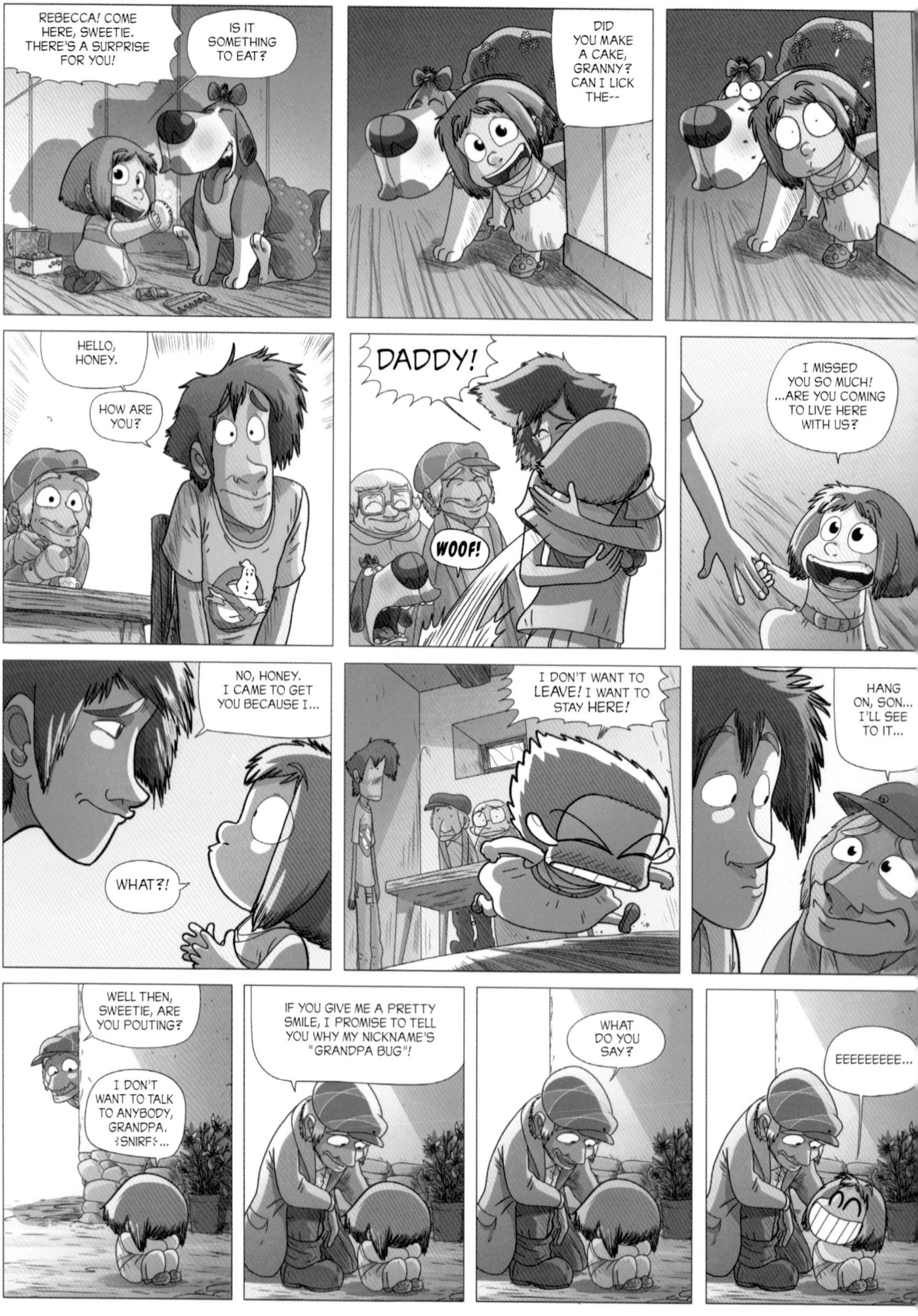
REBECCA! COME HERE, SWEETIE. THERE'S A SURPRISE FOR YOU!
IS IT SOMETHING TO EAT?
DID YOU MAKE A CAKE, GRANNY? CAN I LICK THE--
HELLO, HONEY.
HOW ARE YOU?
DADDY!
WOOF!
I MISSED YOU SO MUCH! ...ARE YOU COMING TO LIVE HERE WITH US?
NO, HONEY. I CAME TO GET YOU BECAUSE I...
WHAT?!
I DON'T WANT TO LEAVE! I WANT TO STAY HERE!
HANG ON, SON... I'LL SEE TO IT...
WELL THEN, SWEETIE, ARE YOU POUTING?
I DON'T WANT TO TALK TO ANYBODY, GRANDPA. ›SNIRF‹...
IF YOU GIVE ME A PRETTY SMILE, I PROMISE TO TELL YOU WHY MY NICKNAME'S "GRANDPA BUG"!
WHAT DO YOU SAY?
EEEEEEEEE...

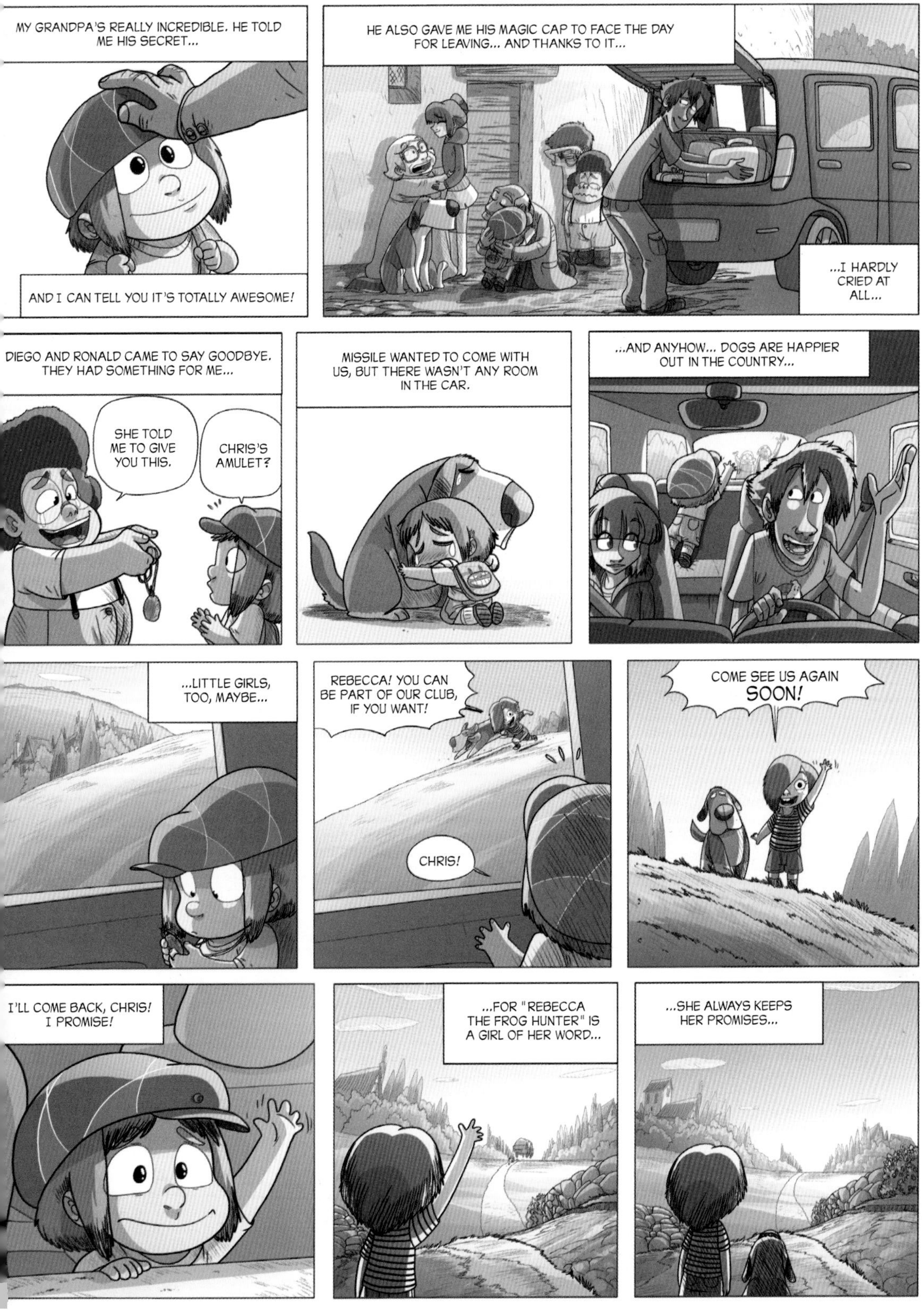
MY GRANDPA'S REALLY INCREDIBLE. HE TOLD ME HIS SECRET...
AND I CAN TELL YOU IT'S TOTALLY AWESOME!
HE ALSO GAVE ME HIS MAGIC CAP TO FACE THE DAY FOR LEAVING... AND THANKS TO IT...
...I HARDLY CRIED AT ALL...
DIEGO AND RONALD CAME TO SAY GOODBYE. THEY HAD SOMETHING FOR ME...
SHE TOLD ME TO GIVE YOU THIS.
CHRIS'S AMULET?
MISSILE WANTED TO COME WITH US, BUT THERE WASN'T ANY ROOM IN THE CAR.
...AND ANYHOW... DOGS ARE HAPPIER OUT IN THE COUNTRY...
...LITTLE GIRLS, TOO, MAYBE...
REBECCA! YOU CAN BE PART OF OUR CLUB, IF YOU WANT!
CHRIS!
COME SEE US AGAIN SOON!
I'LL COME BACK, CHRIS! I PROMISE!
...FOR "REBECCA THE FROG HUNTER" IS A GIRL OF HER WORD...
...SHE ALWAYS KEEPS HER PROMISES...

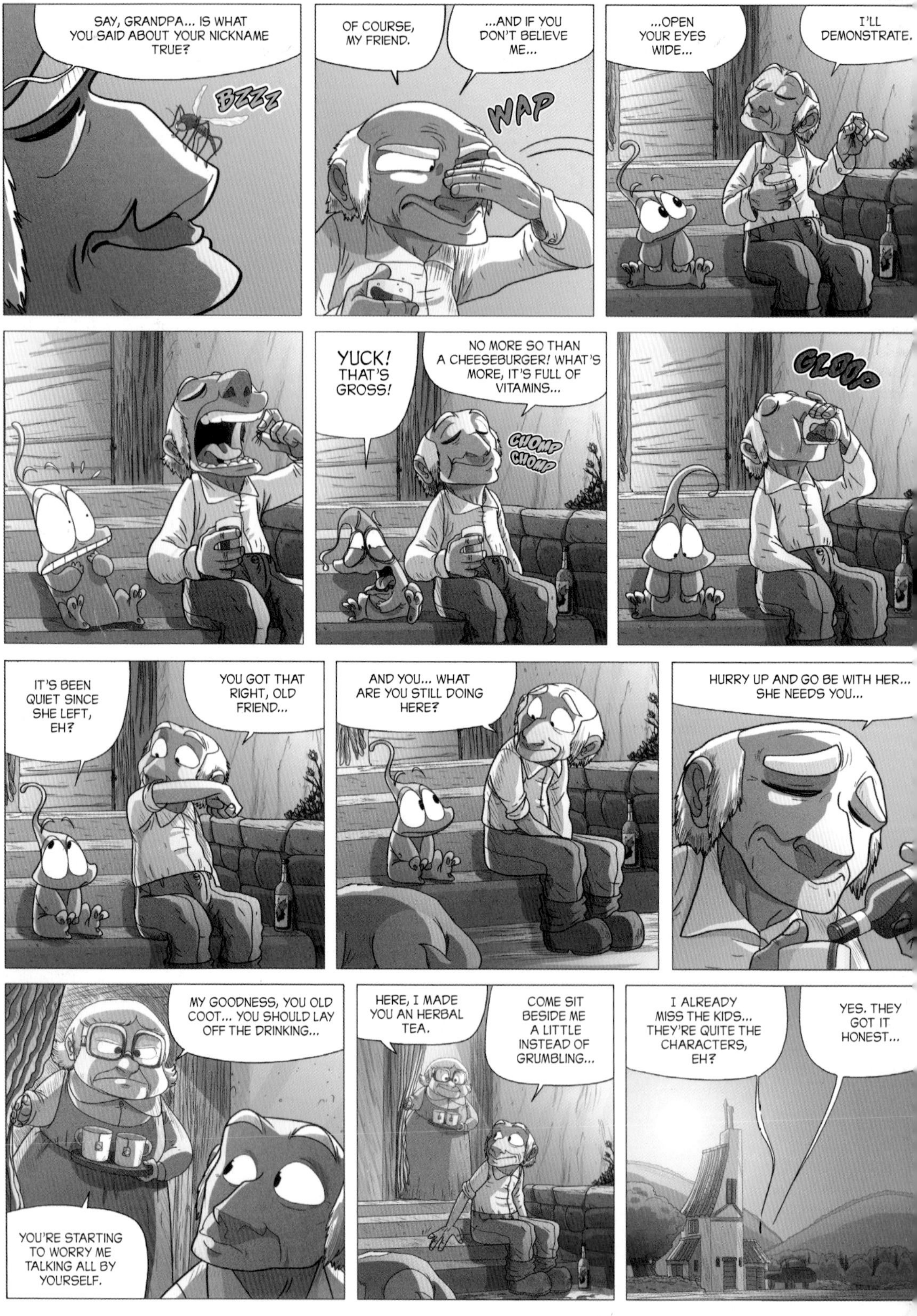
SAY, GRANDPA... IS WHAT YOU SAID ABOUT YOUR NICKNAME TRUE?
BZZZ
OF COURSE, MY FRIEND.
...AND IF YOU DON'T BELIEVE ME...
WAP
...OPEN YOUR EYES WIDE...
I'LL DEMONSTRATE.
YUCK! THAT'S GROSS!
NO MORE SO THAN A CHEESEBURGER! WHAT'S MORE, IT'S FULL OF VITAMINS...
CHOMP CHOMP
GLOUP
IT'S BEEN QUIET SINCE SHE LEFT, EH?
YOU GOT THAT RIGHT, OLD FRIEND...
AND YOU... WHAT ARE YOU STILL DOING HERE?
HURRY UP AND GO BE WITH HER... SHE NEEDS YOU...
MY GOODNESS, YOU OLD COOT... YOU SHOULD LAY OFF THE DRINKING...
YOU'RE STARTING TO WORRY ME TALKING ALL BY YOURSELF.
HERE, I MADE YOU AN HERBAL TEA.
COME SIT BESIDE ME A LITTLE INSTEAD OF GRUMBLING...
I ALREADY MISS THE KIDS... THEY'RE QUITE THE CHARACTERS, EH?
YES. THEY GOT IT HONEST...

WATCH OUT FOR PAPERCUTZ™

Welcome to the third, touchingly transcendent ERNEST & REBECCA graphic novel by Guillaume Bianco and Antonello Dalena. I'm Jim Salicrup, your non-germaphobic Editor-in-Chief of Papercutz, the company dedicated to publishing great graphic novels for all ages. And as I said before, and will probably keep on saying, if ever there was a graphic novel series that's perfect for all ages, it's ERNEST & REBECCA.

Speaking of all ages, you may have noticed that this volume of ERNEST & REBECCA is 6 1/2" x 9" instead of the 8" x 10" size of the first two volumes. The reason is most curious. Turns out that larger books, with lots of pictures in them, are seen as "strictly for kids," by a large segment of our potential audience. In the case of ERNEST & REBECCA, this is further compounded by Rebecca being six and a half years old, as many assume that ERNEST & REBECCA must therefore be intended only for six and a half year olds. To remedy the former, we've reduced the size of the books, while also reducing the price. As for the latter, Rebecca remains six and a half years old, and we hope certain people will come to realize that Guillaume Bianco and Antonello Dalena are producing one of the most well-written and beautifully drawn graphic novels being published today, and understand that stories about children aren't necessarily childish.

As part of our mission to publish great graphic novels, we look at comics from all over the world to find exceptional material that may not be available yet in English. Some of our top titles, such as GERONIMO STILTON and THE SMURFS, were originally created and published in Europe, where many incredible comics are produced. Upon publication, every volume of ERNEST & REBECCA has been made an official Youth Selection of the Angoulême Festival, earning this prestigious honor in 2009, 2010, and 2011. Now, you don't have to be Nancy Drew to surmise that ERNEST & REBECCA was first published in France. One of the biggest clues that Rebecca didn't live in these here parts appeared in ERNEST & REBECCA #2 "Sam the Repulsive," when Rebecca and her dad were pulled over by a police officer:

I AIN'T LITTLE!
WHAT DOES THAT HAIRY SHMURGL WANT?!
THE GENTLEMAN ISN'T A "SHMURGL," REBECCA. HE'S A POLICEMAN.
AND A MUSTACHE IS A KIND OF TRADITION WITH THEM.

Yep, chances are you won't run into that guy on US 1!

A far subtler clue appears in "Grandpa Bug":

SOME CARP LIKE USUAL, GRANDPA BUG?
YES, MY LI'L LUCETTE! AND A NICE ONE! THERE'RE FOUR OF US FOR LUNCH TODAY!

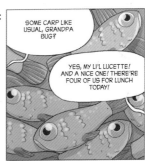

Grandpa Bug actually ordered "some bream," but the bream pictured are a European species of freshwater fish in the carp family that would be very unlikely to be available at a small country market. Likewise, the aioli (a traditional sauce made of garlic, olive oil, and egg) Granny Doodle is preparing on page 31 is far more common in Europe than over here.

Papercutz is proud to publish such great work as ERNEST & REBECCA by Guillaume Bianco and Antonello Dalena. Because we respect the intelligence of our audience, we will continue to publish graphic novels by artists and writers from all over the world— just to bring you the very best comics possible! As we always say, watch out for Papercutz!

WHAT DID YOU SEE?! TELL ME! TELL ME!
QUIET. THE "BACKWARDS OLD WITCH" NEEDS TO CONCENTRATE TO MAKE HER AIOLI...

Thanks,

Jim

SEE ERNEST AND REBECCA AGAIN
VERY SOON IN VOLUME FOUR, TITLED:
"THE LAND OF WALKING STONES."

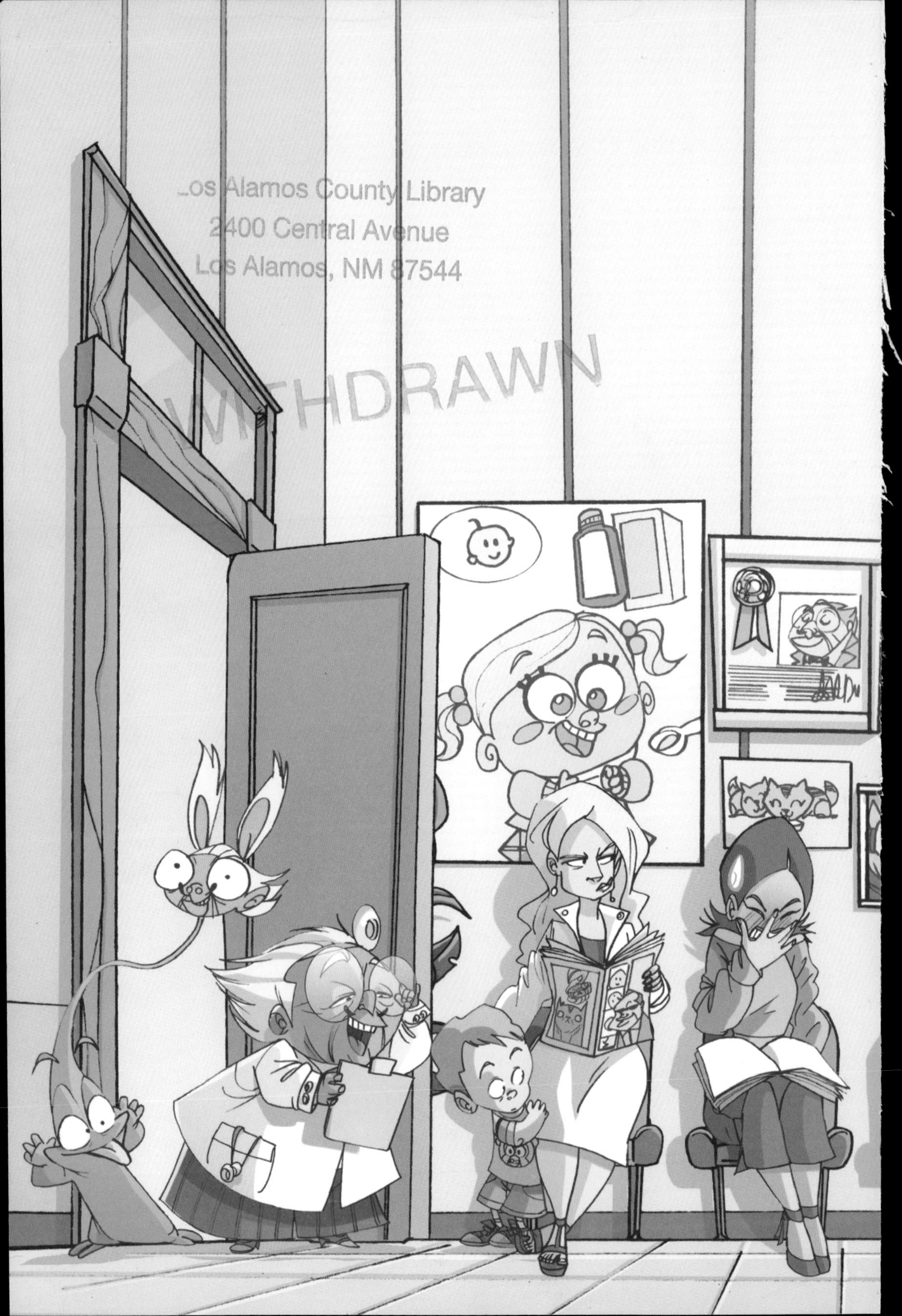